## Praise for the Earthsea Novels
## by Ursula K. Le Guin

"Le Guin, one of modern science fiction's most acclaimed writers, is also a fantasist of genius. . . . [Earthsea] is among her finest creations."
— *New York Times*

"Thrilling, wise and beautiful . . . written in prose as taut and clean as a ship's sail. Every word is perfect."
— *Guardian*

"Among the looms of fantasy fiction, Ursula Le Guin weaves on where J.R.R. Tolkien cast off. . . . Earthsea—fuming with dragons and busy with magic—has replaced Tolkien's Middle Earth as the chosen land for high, other-worldly adventure."
— *Sunday Times* (London)

"Readers will be beguiled by the flawless, poetic prose, the philosophy expressed in thoughtful, potent metaphor, and the consummately imagined world."
— *Kirkus Reviews*

"A thoughtful, brilliant achievement."
— *Horn Book*

"A treasure. . . . It is at the top of any list of fantasy to be cherished."
— award-winning science fiction and fantasy writer Andre Norton

★ "Stellar. . . . Le Guin is still at the height of her powers, a superb stylist with a knack for creating characters who are both wise and deeply humane."
—*Publishers Weekly*, starred review

"Here there be dragons, and Ms. Le Guin's dragons are some of the best in literature."
—award-winning fantasy writer Robin McKinley, *New York Times Book Review*

"Richly told. . . . [Le Guin] draws us into the magical land and its inhabitants' doings immediately."
—*Booklist*

"Strong work from a master storyteller."
—*Library Journal*

"A masterpiece of chilling narration."
—*Guardian*

"All of Ursula Le Guin's strengths are abundantly present . . . narrative power, tautly controlled and responsive prose, an imagination that never loses touch with the reality of things as they are."
—*Economist*

"Le Guin is not only one of the purest stylists writing in English, but the most transcendently truthful of writers."
—*Nation*

"Le Guin understands magic and dragons better than anyone, and her writing only gets better with each new book."
—Michael Stanwick, author of *Stations of the Tide*

# A WIZARD
## OF EARTHSEA

# EARTHSEA

Miles

25 50 100 200 300

Hogen Land

Borth

Sorress

Norst

Eboss kil

Semel

Bish

Ebish

Bosn

Mt Andanden

Hille

Derheman

Narveduen

Paln

Onon

Selidor

Gate of
Selidor

Uly

Risk

Usidero

Ethil

The Dragons' Run

Ingat

Ontuego

Jovet

Seppish

Tonning

Low Tonning

Pendor

The Nine
Isles

The West Reach

Kaltuel

Arrins

Near
Kaltuel

Simly

Faltuel

Ensmer

Serd

Poly

Obb

Jessage

The Sand Isles

Obehol

Lorbanery

The South Reach

The Long Dunes

Wellogy

Far
Sorr

# READ THE EARTHSEA CYCLE:

*A Wizard of Earthsea*
*The Tombs of Atuan*
*The Farthest Shore*
*Tehanu*
*Tales from Earthsea*
*The Other Wind*

AND LOOK FOR ADDITIONAL NOVELS FROM
URSULA K. LE GUIN

# URSULA K. Le GUIN

# A WIZARD OF EARTHSEA

## BOOK ONE OF THE  CYCLE

**G** RAPHIA

**HOUGHTON MIFFLIN HARCOURT**
BOSTON   NEW YORK

*To my brothers*
*Clifton, Ted, Karl*

Copyright © 1968 by Ursula K. Le Guin
Afterword copyright © 2012 by Ursula K. Le Guin

All rights reserved. Published in the United States by Graphia,
an imprint of Houghton Mifflin Harcourt Publishing Company.
Originally published in hardcover in the United States by Houghton
Mifflin Books for Children, an imprint of Houghton Mifflin
Harcourt Publishing Company, 1968.

For information about permission to reproduce selections from this
book, write to trade.permissions@hmhco.com or to Permissions,
Houghton Mifflin Harcourt Publishing Company, 3 Park Avenue,
19th Floor, New York, New York 10016.

Graphia and the Graphia logo are trademarks of Houghton Mifflin
Harcourt Publishing Company.

www.hmhco.com

The text of this book is set in Adobe Garamond.

*Library of Congress Cataloging-in-Publication Data is on file.*

ISBN: 978-0-547-85139-6 hardcover
ISBN: 978-0-547-72202-3 paperback
ISBN: 978-0-547-77374-2 mass market

Printed in the United States of America
DOC 20 19 18 17 16 15 14 13
4500709073

# CONTENTS

Only in silence the word,
only in dark the light,
only in dying life:
bright the hawk's flight
on the empty sky.
—*The Creation of Éa*

# A WIZARD
## OF **EARTHSEA**

# CHAPTER 1

# WARRIORS IN THE MIST

**THE ISLAND OF GONT,** a single mountain that lifts its peak a mile above the storm-racked Northeast Sea, is a land famous for wizards. From the towns in its high valleys and the ports on its dark narrow bays many a Gontishman has gone forth to serve the Lords of the Archipelago in their cities as wizard or mage, or, looking for adventure, to wander working magic from isle to isle of all Earthsea. Of these some say the greatest, and surely the greatest voyager, was the man called Sparrowhawk, who in his day became both dragonlord and Archmage. His life is told of in the *Deed of Ged* and in many songs, but this is a tale of the time before his fame, before the songs were made.

He was born in a lonely village called Ten Alders, high on the mountain at the head of the Northward Vale. Below the village the pastures and plowlands of the Vale slope downward level below level towards the sea, and other towns lie on the bends of the River Ar; above the village only forest rises ridge behind ridge to the stone and snow of the heights.

The name he bore as a child, Duny, was given him by his mother, and that and his life were all she could give him, for she died before he was a year old. His father, the bronze-smith of the village, was a grim unspeaking man, and since Duny's six brothers were older than he by many years and went one by one from home to farm the land or sail the sea or work as smith in other towns of the Northward Vale, there was no one to bring the child up in tenderness. He grew wild, a thriving weed, a tall, quick boy, loud and proud and full of temper. With the few other children of the village he herded goats on the steep meadows above the river-springs; and when he was strong enough to push and pull the long bellows-sleeves, his father made him work as smith's boy, at a high cost in blows and whippings. There was not much work to be got out of Duny. He was always off and away; roaming deep in the forest, swimming in the pools of the River Ar that like all Gontish rivers runs very quick and cold, or climbing by cliff and scarp to the heights above the forest, from which he could see the sea, that broad northern ocean where, past Perregal, no islands are.

A sister of his dead mother lived in the village. She had done what was needful for him as a baby, but she had business of her own and once he could look after himself at all she paid no more heed to him. But one day when the boy was seven years old, untaught and knowing nothing of the arts and powers that are in the world, he heard his aunt crying out words to a goat which had jumped up onto the thatch of a hut and would not come down: but it came jumping when she cried a certain rhyme to it. Next day herding the longhaired goats on the meadows of High Fall, Duny shouted to them the words he had heard, not knowing their use or meaning or what kind of words they were:

> *Noth hierth malk man*
> *hiolk han merth han!*

He yelled the rhyme aloud, and the goats came to him. They came very quickly, all of them together, not making any sound. They looked at him out of the dark slot in their yellow eyes.

Duny laughed and shouted it out again, the rhyme that gave him power over the goats. They came closer, crowding and pushing round him. All at once he felt afraid of their thick, ridged horns and their strange eyes and their strange silence. He tried to get free of them and to run away. The goats ran with him keeping in a knot around him, and so they came charging down into the village at last, all the goats going huddled together as if a rope were pulled tight round them, and the boy in the midst of them weeping and bellowing. Villagers ran from their houses to swear at the goats and laugh at the boy. Among them came the boy's aunt, who did not laugh. She said a word to the goats, and the beasts began to bleat and browse and wander, freed from the spell.

"Come with me," she said to Duny.

She took him into her hut where she lived alone. She let no child enter there usually, and the children feared the place. It was low and dusky, windowless, fragrant with herbs that hung drying from the crosspole of the roof, mint and moly and thyme, yarrow and rushwash and paramal, kingsfoil, clovenfoot, tansy and bay. There his aunt sat crosslegged by the firepit, and looking sidelong at the boy through the tangles of her black hair she asked him what he had said to the goats, and if he knew what the rhyme was. When she found that he knew nothing, and yet had spellbound the goats to come to him and follow him, then she saw that he must have in him the makings of power.

As her sister's son he had been nothing to her, but now she looked at him with a new eye. She praised him, and told him she might teach him rhymes he would like better, such as the word that makes a snail look out of its shell, or the name that calls a falcon down from the sky.

"Aye, teach me that name!" he said, being clear over the fright the goats had given him, and puffed up with her praise of his cleverness.

The witch said to him, "You will not ever tell that word to the other children, if I teach it to you."

"I promise."

She smiled at his ready ignorance. "Well and good. But I will bind your promise. Your tongue will be stilled until I choose to unbind it, and even then, though you can speak, you will not be able to speak the word I teach you where another person can hear it. We must keep the secrets of our craft."

"Good," said the boy, for he had no wish to tell the secret to his playmates, liking to know and do what they knew not and could not.

He sat still while his aunt bound back her uncombed hair, and knotted the belt of her dress, and again sat cross-legged throwing handfuls of leaves into the firepit, so that a smoke spread and filled the darkness of the hut. She began to sing. Her voice changed sometimes to low or high as if another voice sang through her, and the singing went on and on until the boy did not know if he waked or slept, and all the while the witch's old black dog that never barked sat by him with eyes red from the smoke. Then the witch spoke to Duny in a tongue he did not understand, and made him say with her certain rhymes and words until the enchantment came on him and held him still.

"Speak!" she said to test the spell.

The boy could not speak, but he laughed.

Then his aunt was a little afraid of his strength, for this was as strong a spell as she knew how to weave: she had tried not only to gain control of his speech and silence, but to bind him at the same time to her service in the craft of sorcery. Yet even as the spell bound him, he had laughed. She said nothing. She threw clear water on the fire till the smoke cleared away, and gave the boy water to drink, and when the air was clear and he could speak again she taught him the true name of the falcon, to which the falcon must come.

This was Duny's first step on the way he was to follow all his life, the way of magery, the way that led him at last to hunt a shadow over land and sea to the lightless coasts of death's kingdom. But in those first steps along the way, it seemed a broad, bright road.

When he found that the wild falcons stooped down to him from the wind when he summoned them by name, lighting with a thunder of wings on his wrist like the hunting-birds of a prince, then he hungered to know more such names and came to his aunt begging to learn the name of the sparrowhawk and the osprey and the eagle. To earn the words of power he did all the witch asked of him and learned of her all she taught, though not all of it was pleasant to do or know. There is a saying on Gont, *Weak as woman's magic*, and there is another saying, *Wicked as woman's magic*. Now the witch of Ten Alders was no black sorceress, nor did she ever meddle with the high arts or traffic with Old Powers; but being an ignorant woman among ignorant folk, she often used her crafts to foolish and dubious ends. She knew nothing of the Balance and the Pattern which the true wizard knows and serves, and which keep him from using his spells unless real need demands. She had a spell for every circumstance, and was forever weaving charms. Much of her lore was mere rubbish and humbug, nor did she know the true spells from the false. She knew many curses, and was better at causing sickness, perhaps, than at curing it. Like any village witch she could brew up a love-potion, but there were other, uglier brews she made to serve men's jealousy and hate. Such practices, however, she kept from her young prentice, and as far as she was able she taught him honest craft.

At first all his pleasure in the art-magic was, childlike, the power it gave him over bird and beast, and the knowledge of these. And indeed that plea-

sure stayed with him all his life. Seeing him in the
high pastures often with a bird of prey about him,
the other children called him Sparrowhawk, and so
he came by the name that he kept in later life as his
use-name, when his true-name was not known.

As the witch kept talking of the glory and the
riches and the great power over men that a sorcerer
could gain, he set himself to learn more useful lore.
He was very quick at it. The witch praised him and
the children of the village began to fear him, and
he himself was sure that very soon he would become great among men. So he went on from word
to word and from spell to spell with the witch till
he was twelve years old and had learned from her a
great part of what she knew: not much, but enough
for the witchwife of a small village, and more than
enough for a boy of twelve. She had taught him all
her lore in herbals and healing, and all she knew
of the crafts of finding, binding, mending, un-
sealing and revealing. What she knew of chanters'
tales and the great Deeds she had sung him, and all
the words of the True Speech that she had learned
from the sorcerer that taught her, she taught again
to Duny. And from weatherworkers and wandering jugglers who went from town to town of the
Northward Vale and the East Forest he had learned
various tricks and pleasantries, spells of Illusion.

It was with one of these light spells that he first proved the great power that was in him.

In those days the Kargad Empire was strong. Those are four great lands that lie between the Northern and the Eastern Reaches: Karego-At, Atuan, Hur-at-Hur, Atnini. The tongue they speak there is not like any spoken in the Archipelago or the other Reaches, and they are a savage people, white-skinned, yellow-haired, and fierce, liking the sight of blood and the smell of burning towns. Last year they had attacked the Torikles and the strong island Torheven, raiding in great force in fleets of red-sailed ships. News of this came north to Gont, but the Lords of Gont were busy with their piracy and paid small heed to the woes of other lands. Then Spevy fell to the Kargs and was looted and laid waste, its people taken as slaves, so that even now it is an isle of ruins. In lust of conquest the Kargs sailed next to Gont, coming in a host, thirty great longships, to East Port. They fought through that town, took it, burned it; leaving their ships under guard at the mouth of the River Ar they went up the Vale wrecking and looting, slaughtering cattle and men. As they went they split into bands, and each of these bands plundered where it chose. Fugitives brought warning to the villages of the heights. Soon the people of Ten Alders saw smoke darken the eastern sky, and that night those who climbed the High Fall looked down on the Vale all hazed and red-streaked with fires where fields ready for harvest had been set ablaze, and orchards burned, the fruit roasting on the blazing boughs, and barns and farmhouses smoldered in ruin.

Some of the villagers fled up the ravines and hid in the forest, and some made ready to fight for their lives, and some did neither but stood about lamenting. The witch was one who fled, hiding alone in a cave up on the Kapperding Scarp and sealing the cave-mouth with spells. Duny's father the bronze-smith was one who stayed, for he would not leave his smelting-pit and forge where he had worked for fifty years. All that night he labored beating up what ready metal he had there into spear-points, and others worked with him binding these to the handles of hoes and rakes, there being no time to make sockets and shaft them properly. There had been no weapons in the village but hunting bows and short knives, for the mountain folk of Gont are not warlike; it is not warriors they are famous for, but goat-thieves, sea-pirates, and wizards.

With sunrise came a thick white fog, as on many autumn mornings in the heights of the island. Among their huts and houses down the straggling street of Ten Alders the villagers stood waiting with their hunting bows and new-forged spears, not knowing whether the Kargs might be far off or very near, all silent, all peering into the fog that hid shapes and distances and dangers from their eyes.

With them was Duny. He had worked all night at the forge-bellows, pushing and pulling the two long sleeves of goathide that fed the fire with a blast of air. Now his arms so ached and trembled from that work that he could not hold out the spear he had chosen. He did not see how he could fight or be of any good to himself or the villagers. It rankled at his heart that he should die, spitted on a Kargish lance, while still a boy: that he should go into the dark land without ever having known his own name, his true name as a man. He looked down at his thin arms, wet with cold fog-dew, and raged at his weakness, for he knew his strength. There was power in him, if he knew how to use it, and he sought among all the spells he knew for some device that might give him and his companions an advantage, or at least a chance. But need alone is not enough to set power free: there must be knowledge.

The fog was thinning now under the heat of the sun that shone bare above on the peak in a bright sky. As the mists moved and parted in great drifts and smoky wisps, the villagers saw a band of warriors coming up the mountain. They were armored with bronze helmets and greaves and breastplates of heavy leather and shields of wood and bronze, and armed with swords and the long Kargish lance. Winding up along the steep bank of the Ar they came in a plumed, clanking, straggling line, near enough already that their white faces could be seen, and the words of their jargon heard as they shouted to one another. In this band of the invading horde there were about a hundred men, which is not many; but in the village were only eighteen men and boys.

Now need called knowledge out: Duny, seeing the fog blow and thin across the path before the Kargs, saw a spell that might avail him. An old weatherworker of the Vale, seeking to win the boy as prentice, had taught him several charms. One of these tricks was called fogweaving, a binding-spell that gathers the mists together for a while in one place; with it one skilled in illusion can shape the mist into fair ghostly seemings, which last a little and fade away. The boy had no such skill, but his intent was different, and he had the strength to turn the spell to his own ends. Rapidly and aloud he named the places and the boundaries of the village, and then spoke the fogweaving charm, but in among its words he enlaced the words of a spell of concealment, and last he cried the word that set the magic going.

Even as he did so his father coming up behind him struck him hard on the side of the head, knocking him right down. "Be still, fool! Keep your blattering mouth shut, and hide if you can't fight!"

Duny got to his feet. He could hear the Kargs now at the end of the village, as near as the great yew-tree by the tanner's yard. Their voices were clear, and the clink and creak of their harness and arms, but they could not be seen. The fog had closed and thickened all over the village, greying the light, blurring the world till a man could hardly see his own hands before him.

"I've hidden us all," Duny said, sullenly, for his head hurt from his father's blow, and the working of the doubled incantation had drained his strength. "I'll keep up this fog as long as I can. Get the others to lead them up to High Fall."

The smith stared at his son who stood wraith-like in that weird, dank mist. It took him a minute to see Duny's meaning, but when he did he ran at once, noiselessly, knowing every fence and corner of the village, to find the others and tell them what to do. Now through the grey fog bloomed a blur of red, as the Kargs set fire to the thatch of a house. Still they did not come up into the village, but waited at the lower end till the mist should lift and lay bare their loot and prey.

The tanner, whose house it was that burned, sent a couple of boys skipping right under the Kargs' noses, taunting and yelling and vanishing again like smoke into smoke. Meantime the older men, creeping behind fences and running from house to house, came close on the other side and sent a volley of arrows and spears at the warriors, who stood all in a bunch. One Karg fell writhing with a spear, still warm from its forging, right through his body. Others were arrow-bitten, and all enraged. They charged forward then to hew down their puny attackers, but they found only the fog about them, full of voices. They followed the voices, stabbing ahead into the mist with their great, plumed, bloodstained lances. Up the length of the street they came shouting, and never knew they had run right through the village, as the empty huts and houses loomed and disappeared again in the writhing grey fog. The villagers ran scattering, most of them keeping well ahead since they knew the ground; but some, boys or old men, were slow. The Kargs stumbling on them drove their lances or hacked with their swords, yelling their war-cry, the names of the White Godbrothers of Atuan:

"Wuluah! Atwah!"

Some of the band stopped when they felt the land grow rough underfoot, but others pressed right on, seeking the phantom village, following

dim wavering shapes that fled just out of reach before them. All the mist had come alive with these
fleeting forms, dodging, flickering, fading on every
side. One group of the Kargs chased the wraiths
straight to the High Fall, the cliff's edge above the
springs of Ar, and the shapes they pursued ran out
onto the air and there vanished in a thinning of
the mist, while the pursuers fell screaming through
fog and sudden sunlight a hundred feet sheer to
the shallow pools among the rocks. And those that
came behind and did not fall stood at the cliff's
edge, listening.

Now dread came into the Kargs' hearts and
they began to seek one another, not the villagers,
in the uncanny mist. They gathered on the hillside, and yet always there were wraiths and ghost-
shapes among them, and other shapes that ran and
stabbed from behind with spear or knife and vanished again. The Kargs began to run, all of them,
downhill, stumbling, silent, until all at once they
ran out from the grey blind mist and saw the river
and the ravines below the village all bare and bright
in morning sunlight. Then they stopped, gathering together, and looked back. A wall of wavering,
writhing grey lay blank across the path, hiding all
that lay behind it. Out from it burst two or three
stragglers, lunging and stumbling along, their long
lances rocking on their shoulders. Not one Karg

looked back more than that once. All went down, in haste, away from the enchanted place.

Farther down the Northward Vale those warriors got their fill of fighting. The towns of the East Forest, from Ovark to the coast, had gathered their men and sent them against the invaders of Gont. Band after band they came down from the hills, and that day and the next the Kargs were harried back down to the beaches above East Port, where they found their ships burnt; so they fought with their backs to the sea till every man of them was killed, and the sands of Armouth were brown with blood until the tide came in.

But on that morning in Ten Alders village and up on the High Fall, the dank grey fog had clung a while, and then suddenly it blew and drifted and melted away. This man and that stood up in the windy brightness of the morning, and looked about him wondering. Here lay a dead Karg with yellow hair long, loose, and bloody; there lay the village tanner, killed in battle like a king.

Down in the village the house that had been set afire still blazed. They ran to put the fire out, since their battle had been won. In the street, near the great yew, they found Duny the bronze-smith's son standing by himself, bearing no hurt, but speechless and stupid like one stunned. They were well aware of what he had done, and they led him into

as prentice, or see to it that he is schooled as fits his gifts. For to keep dark the mind of the mageborn, that is a dangerous thing."

Very gently Ogion spoke, but with certainty, and even the hardheaded smith assented to all he said.

On the day the boy was thirteen years old, a day in the early splendor of autumn while still the bright leaves are on the trees, Ogion returned to the village from his rovings over Gont Mountain, and the ceremony of Passage was held. The witch took from the boy his name Duny, the name his mother had given him as a baby. Nameless and naked he walked into the cold springs of the Ar where it rises among rocks under the high cliffs. As he entered the water clouds crossed the sun's face and great shadows slid and mingled over the water of the pool about him. He crossed to the far bank, shuddering with cold but walking slow and erect as he should through that icy, living water. As he came to the bank Ogion, waiting, reached out his hand and clasping the boy's arm whispered to him his true name: Ged.

Thus was he given his name by one very wise in the uses of power.

The feasting was far from over, and all the villagers were making merry with plenty to eat and beer to drink and a chanter from down the Vale singing the *Deed of the Dragonlords,* when the mage spoke in his quiet voice to Ged: "Come, lad. Bid your people farewell and leave them feasting."

Ged fetched what he had to carry, which was the good bronze knife his father had forged him, and a leather coat the tanner's widow had cut down to his size, and an alder-stick his aunt had becharmed for him: that was all he owned besides his shirt and breeches. He said farewell to them, all the people he knew in all the world, and looked about once at the village that straggled and huddled there under the cliffs, over the riversprings. Then he set off with his new master through the steep slanting forests of the mountain isle, through the leaves and shadows of bright autumn.

# CHAPTER 2

# THE SHADOW

GED HAD THOUGHT THAT AS the prentice of a great mage he would enter at once into the mystery and mastery of power. He would understand the language of the beasts and the speech of the leaves of the forest, he thought, and sway the winds with his word, and learn to change himself into any shape he wished. Maybe he and his master would run together as stags, or fly to Re Albi over the mountain on the wings of eagles.

But it was not so at all. They wandered, first down into the Vale and then gradually south and westward around the mountain, given lodging in little villages or spending the night out in the wilderness, like poor journeyman-sorcerers, or tinkers, or beggars. They entered no mysterious domain. Nothing happened. The mage's oaken staff that Ged had watched at first with eager dread was nothing but a stout staff to walk with. Three days went by and four days went by and still Ogion had not spoken a single charm in Ged's hearing, and had not taught him a single name or rune or spell.

Though a very silent man he was so mild and calm that Ged soon lost his awe of him, and in a day or two more he was bold enough to ask his master, "When will my apprenticeship begin, Sir?"

"It has begun," said Ogion.

There was a silence, as if Ged was keeping back something he had to say. Then he said it: "But I haven't learned anything yet!"

"Because you haven't found out what I am teaching," replied the mage, going on at his steady, long-legged pace along their road, which was the high pass between Ovark and Wiss. He was a dark man, like most Gontishmen, dark copper-brown; grey-haired, lean and tough as a hound, tireless. He spoke seldom, ate little, slept less. His eyes and ears were very keen, and often there was a listening look on his face.

Ged did not answer him. It is not always easy to answer a mage.

"You want to work spells," Ogion said presently, striding along. "You've drawn too much water from that well. Wait. Manhood is patience. Mastery is nine times patience. What is that herb by the path?"

"Strawflower."

"And that?"

"I don't know."

"Fourfoil, they call it." Ogion had halted, the coppershod foot of his staff near the little weed, so Ged looked closely at the plant, and plucked a dry seedpod from it, and finally asked, since Ogion said nothing more, "What is its use, Master?"

"None I know of."

Ged kept the seedpod a while as they went on, then tossed it away.

"When you know the fourfoil in all its seasons root and leaf and flower, by sight and scent and seed, then you may learn its true name, knowing its being: which is more than its use. What, after all, is the use of you? or of myself? Is Gont Mountain useful, or the Open Sea?" Ogion went on a half mile or so, and said at last, "To hear, one must be silent."

The boy frowned. He did not like to be made to feel a fool. He kept back his resentment and impatience, and tried to be obedient, so that Ogion would consent at last to teach him something. For he hungered to learn, to gain power. It began to seem to him, though, that he could have learned more walking with any herb-gatherer or village sorcerer, and as they went round the mountain westward into the lonely forests past Wiss he wondered more and more what was the greatness and the magic of this great Mage Ogion. For when it rained Ogion would not even say the spell that ev-

ery weatherworker knows, to send the storm aside.
In a land where sorcerers come thick, like Gont or
the Enlades, you may see a raincloud blundering
slowly from side to side and place to place as one
spell shunts it on to the next, till at last it is buf-
feted out over the sea where it can rain in peace.
But Ogion let the rain fall where it would. He
found a thick fir-tree and lay down beneath it. Ged
crouched among the dripping bushes wet and sullen, and wondered what was the good of having
power if you were too wise to use it, and wished he
had gone as prentice to that old weatherworker of
the Vale, where at least he would have slept dry. He
did not speak any of his thoughts aloud. He said
not a word. His master smiled, and fell asleep in
the rain.

Along towards Sunreturn when the first heavy
snows began to fall in the heights of Gont they
came to Re Albi, Ogion's home. It is a town on the
edge of the high rocks of Overfell, and its name
means Falcon's Nest. From it one can see far below
the deep harbor and the towers of the Port of Gont,
and the ships that go in and out the gate of the
bay between the Armed Cliffs, and far to the west
across the sea one may make out the blue hills of
Oranéa, easternmost of the Inward Isles.

The mage's house, though large and soundly
built of timber, with hearth and chimney rather

than a firepit, was like the huts of Ten Alders village: all one room, with a goatshed built onto one side. There was a kind of alcove in the west wall of the room, where Ged slept. Over his pallet was a window that looked out on the sea, but most often the shutters must be closed against the great winds that blew all winter from the west and north. In the dark warmth of that house Ged spent the winter, hearing the rush of rain and wind outside or the silence of snowfall, learning to write and read the Six Hundred Runes of Hardic. Very glad he was to learn this lore, for without it no mere rote-learning of charms and spells will give a man true mastery. The Hardic tongue of the Archipelago, though it has no more magic power in it than any other tongue of men, has its roots in the Old Speech, that language in which things are named with their true names: and the way to the understanding of this speech starts with the Runes that were written when the islands of the world first were raised up from the sea.

Still no marvels and enchantments occurred. All winter there was nothing but the heavy pages of the Runebook turning, and the rain and the snow falling; and Ogion would come in from roaming the icy forests or from looking after his goats, and stamp the snow off his boots, and sit down in silence by the fire. And the mage's long, listening

silence would fill the room, and fill Ged's mind,
until sometimes it seemed he had forgotten what
words sounded like: and when Ogion spoke at last
it was as if he had, just then and for the first time,
invented speech. Yet the words he spoke were no
great matters but had to do only with simple things,
bread and water and weather and sleep.

As the spring came on, quick and bright, Ogion
often sent Ged forth to gather herbs on the meadows above Re Albi, and told him to take as long as
he liked about it, giving him freedom to spend all
day wandering by rain-filled streams and through
the woods and over wet green fields in the sun.
Ged went with delight each time, and stayed out
till night; but he did not entirely forget the herbs.
He kept an eye out for them, while he climbed
and roamed and waded and explored, and always
brought some home. He came on a meadow between two streams where the flower called white
hallows grew thick, and as these blossoms are rare
and prized by healers, he came back again next day.
Someone else was there before him, a girl, whom
he knew by sight as the daughter of the old Lord of
Re Albi. He would not have spoken to her, but she
came to him and greeted him pleasantly: "I know
you, you are the Sparrowhawk, our mage's adept. I
wish you would tell me about sorcery!"

He looked down at the white flowers that

brushed against her white skirt, and at first he was shy and glum and hardly answered. But she went on talking, in an open, careless, willful way that little by little set him at ease. She was a tall girl of about his own age, very sallow, almost white-skinned; her mother, they said in the village, was from Osskil or some such foreign land. Her hair fell long and straight like a fall of black water. Ged thought her very ugly, but he had a desire to please her, to win her admiration, that grew on him as they talked. She made him tell all the story of his tricks with the mist that had defeated the Kargish warriors, and she listened as if she wondered and admired, but she spoke no praise. And soon she was off on another tack: "Can you call the birds and beasts to you?" she asked.

"I can," said Ged.

He knew there was a falcon's nest in the cliffs above the meadow, and he summoned the bird by its name. It came, but it would not light on his wrist, being put off no doubt by the girl's presence. It screamed and struck the air with broad barred wings, and rose up on the wind.

"What do you call that kind of charm, that made the falcon come?"

"A spell of Summoning."

"Can you call the spirits of the dead to come to you, too?"

He thought she was mocking him with this question, because the falcon had not fully obeyed his summons. He would not let her mock him. "I might if I chose," he said in a calm voice.

"Is it not very difficult, very dangerous, to summon a spirit?"

"Difficult, yes. Dangerous?" He shrugged.

This time he was almost certain there was admiration in her eyes.

"Can you make a love-charm?"

"That is no mastery."

"True," says she, "any village witch can do it. Can you do Changing spells? Can you change your own shape, as wizards do, they say?"

Again he was not quite sure that she did not ask the question mockingly, and so again he replied, "I might if I chose."

She began to beg him to transform himself into anything he wished—a hawk, a bull, a fire, a tree. He put her off with short secretive words such as his master used, but he did not know how to refuse flatly when she coaxed him; and besides he did not know whether he himself believed his boast, or not. He left her, saying that his master the mage expected him at home, and he did not come back to the meadow the next day. But the day after he came again, saying to himself that he should gather more of the flowers while they bloomed. She was there, and together they waded barefoot in the boggy grass, pulling the heavy white hallow-blooms. The sun of spring shone, and she talked with him as merrily as any goatherd lass of his own village. She asked him again about sorcery, and listened wide-eyed to all he told her, so that he fell to boasting again. Then she asked him if he would not work a Changing spell, and when he put her off, she looked at him, putting back the black hair from her face, and said, "Are you afraid to do it?"

"No, I am not afraid."

She smiled a little disdainfully and said, "Maybe you are too young."

That he would not endure. He did not say much, but he resolved that he would prove himself to her. He told her to come again to the meadow tomorrow, if she liked, and so took leave of her, and came back to the house while his master was still out. He went straight to the shelf and took down the two Lore-Books, which Ogion had never yet opened in his presence.

He looked for a spell of self-transformation, but being slow to read the runes yet and understanding little of what he read, he could not find what he sought. These books were very ancient, Ogion having them from his own master Heleth Farseer, and Heleth from his master the Mage of Perregal, and so back into the times of myth. Small and strange was the writing, overwritten and interlined by many hands, and all those hands were dust now. Yet here and there Ged understood something of what he tried to read, and with the girl's questions and her mockery always in his mind, he stopped on a page that bore a spell of summoning up the spirits of the dead.

As he read it, puzzling out the runes and symbols one by one, a horror came over him. His eyes were fixed, and he could not lift them till he had finished reading all the spell.

Then raising his head he saw it was dark in the house. He had been reading without any light, in the darkness. He could not now make out the runes when he looked down at the book. Yet the horror grew in him, seeming to hold him bound in his chair. He was cold. Looking over his shoulder he saw that something was crouching beside the closed door, a shapeless clot of shadow darker than the darkness. It seemed to reach out towards him, and to whisper, and to call to him in a whisper: but he could not understand the words.

The door was flung wide. A man entered with a white light flaming about him, a great bright figure who spoke aloud, fiercely and suddenly. The darkness and the whispering ceased and were dispelled.

The horror went out of Ged, but still he was

mortally afraid, for it was Ogion the Mage who stood there in the doorway with a brightness all about him, and the oaken staff in his hand burned with a white radiance.

Saying no word the mage came past Ged, and lighted the lamp, and put the books away on their shelf. Then he turned to the boy and said, "You will never work that spell but in peril of your power and your life. Was it for that spell you opened the books?"

"No, Master," the boy murmured, and shamefully he told Ogion what he had sought, and why.

"You do not remember what I told you, that that girl's mother, the Lord's wife, is an enchantress?"

Indeed Ogion had once said this, but Ged had not paid much attention, though he knew by now that Ogion never told him anything that he had not good reason to tell him.

"The girl herself is half a witch already. It may be the mother who sent the girl to talk to you. It may be she who opened the book to the page you read. The powers she serves are not the powers I serve: I do not know her will, but I know she does not will me well. Ged, listen to me now. Have you never thought how danger must surround power as shadow does light? This sorcery is not a game we play for pleasure or for praise. Think of this: that every word, every act of our Art is said and is done either for good, or for evil. Before you speak or do you must know the price that is to pay!"

Driven by his shame Ged cried, "How am I to know these things, when you teach me nothing? Since I lived with you I have done nothing, seen nothing—"

"Now you have seen something," said the mage. "By the door, in the darkness, when I came in."

Ged was silent.

Ogion knelt down and built the fire on the hearth and lit it, for the house was cold. Then still kneeling he said in his quiet voice, "Ged, my young falcon, you are not bound to me or to my service. You did not come to me, but I to you. You are very young to make this choice, but I cannot make it for you. If you wish, I will send you to Roke Island, where all high arts are taught. Any craft you undertake to learn you will learn, for your power is great. Greater even than your pride, I hope. I would keep you here with me, for what I have is what you lack, but I will not keep you against your will. Now choose between Re Albi and Roke."

Ged stood dumb, his heart bewildered. He had to love this man Ogion who had healed him touch, and who had no anger: he loved him, not known it until now. He looked at the f leaning in the chimney-corner, remem-

bering the radiance of it that had burned out evil
from the dark, and he yearned to stay with Ogion,
to go wandering through the forests with him, long
and far, learning how to be silent. Yet other crav-
ings were in him that would not be stilled, the wish
for glory, the will to act. Ogion's seemed a long road
towards mastery, a slow bypath to follow, when he
might go sailing before the seawinds straight to the
Inmost Sea, to the Isle of the Wise, where the air
was bright with enchantments and the Archmage
walked amidst wonders.

"Master," he said, "I will go to Roke."

So a few days later on a sunny morning of spring
Ogion strode beside him down the steep road from
the Overfell, fifteen miles to the Great Port of Gont.
There at the landgate between carven dragons the
guards of the City of Gont, seeing the mage, knelt
with bared swords and welcomed him. They knew
him and did him honor by the Prince's order and
their own will, for ten years ago Ogion had saved
the city from earthquake that would have shaken
the towers of the rich down to the ground and
closed the channel of the Armed Cliffs with avalanche. He had spoken to the Mountain of Gont,
calming it, and had stilled the trembling precipices
of the Overfell as one soothes a frightened beast.
Ged had heard some talk of this, and now, wondering to see the armed guardsmen kneel to his quiet

master, he remembered it. He glanced up almost in
fear at this man who had stopped an earthquake;
but Ogion's face was quiet as always.

They went down to the quays, where the Harbormaster came hastening to welcome Ogion and
ask what service he might do. The mage told him,
and at once he named a ship bound for the Inmost
Sea aboard which Ged might go as passenger. "Or
they will take him as windbringer," he said, "if he
has the craft. They have no weatherworker aboard."

"He has some skill with mist and fog, but none
with seawinds," the mage said, putting his hand
lightly on Ged's shoulder. "Do not try any tricks
with the sea and the winds of the sea, Sparrowhawk; you are a landsman still. Harbormaster,
what is the ship's name?"

"*Shadow,* from the Andrades, bound to Hort
Town with furs and ivories. A good ship, Master
Ogion."

The mage's face darkened at the name of the
ship, but he said, "So be it. Give this writing to the
Warder of the School on Roke, Sparrowhawk. Go
with a fair wind. Farewell!"

That was all his parting. He turned away, and
went striding up the street away from the quays.
Ged stood forlorn and watched his master go.

"Come along, lad," said the Harbormaster, and

took him down the waterfront to the pier where *Shadow* was making ready to sail.

It might seem strange that on an island fifty miles wide, in a village under cliffs that stare out forever on the sea, a child may grow to manhood never having stepped in a boat or dipped his finger in salt water, but so it is. Farmer, goatherd, cattle-herd, hunter or artisan, the landsman looks at the ocean as at a salt unsteady realm that has nothing to do with him at all. The village two days' walk from his village is a foreign land, and the island a day's sail from his island is a mere rumor, misty hills seen across the water, not solid ground like that he walks on.

So to Ged who had never been down from the heights of the mountain, the Port of Gont was an awesome and marvellous place, the great houses and towers of cut stone and waterfront of piers and docks and basins and moorages, the seaport where half a hundred boats and galleys rocked at quay-side or lay hauled up and overturned for repairs or stood out at anchor in the roadstead with furled sails and closed oarports, the sailors shouting in strange dialects and the longshoremen running heavy-laden amongst barrels and boxes and coils of rope and stacks of oars, the bearded merchants in furred robes conversing quietly as they picked their

way along the slimy stones above the water, the
fishermen unloading their catch, coopers pound-
ing and shipmakers hammering and clamsellers
singing and shipmasters bellowing, and beyond
all the silent, shining bay. With eyes and ears and
mind bewildered he followed the Harbormaster to
the broad dock where *Shadow* was tied up, and the
Harbormaster brought him to the master of the
ship.

With few words spoken the ship's master agreed
to take Ged as passenger to Roke, since it was a
mage that asked it; and the Harbormaster left the
boy with him. The master of the *Shadow* was a big
man, and fat, in a red cloak trimmed with pellawi-
fur such as Andradean merchants wear. He never
looked at Ged but asked him in a mighty voice,
"Can you work weather, boy?"

"I can."

"Can you bring the wind?"

He had to say he could not, and with that the
master told him to find a place out of the way and
stay in it.

The oarsmen were coming aboard now, for the
ship was to go out into the roadstead before night
fell, and sail with the ebbtide near dawn. There
was no place out of the way, but Ged climbed up
as well as he could onto the bundled, lashed, and
hide-covered cargo in the stern of the ship, and

clinging there watched all that passed. The oarsmen came leaping aboard, sturdy men with great
arms, while longshoremen rolled water barrels
thundering out the dock and stowed them under
the rowers' benches. The well-built ship rode low
with her burden, yet danced a little on the lapping
shore-waves, ready to be gone. Then the steersman
took his place at the right of the sternpost, looking forward to the ship's master, who stood on a
plank let in at the jointure of the keel with the stem,
which was carved as the Old Serpent of Andrad.
The master roared his orders hugely, and *Shadow*
was untied and towed clear of the docks by two
laboring rowboats. Then the master's roar was
"Open ports!" and the great oars shot rattling out,
fifteen to a side. The rowers bent their strong backs
while a lad up beside the master beat the stroke on
a drum. Easy as a gull oared by her wings the ship
went now, and the noise and hurlyburly of the City
fell away suddenly behind. They came out in the
silence of the waters of the bay, and over them rose
the white peak of the Mountain, seeming to hang
above the sea. In a shallow creek in the lee of the
southern Armed Cliff the anchor was thrown over,
and there they rode the night.

Of the seventy crewmen of the ship some were
like Ged very young in years, though all had made
their passage into manhood. These lads called him

over to share food and drink with them, and were friendly though rough and full of jokes and jibes. They called him Goatherd, of course, because he was Gontish, but they did not go further than that. He was as tall and strong as the fifteen-year-olds, and quick to return either a good word or a jeer; so he made his way among them and even that first night began to live as one of them and learn their work. This suited the ship's officers, for there was no room aboard for idle passengers.

There was little enough room for the crew, and no comfort at all, in an undecked galley crowded with men and gear and cargo; but what was comfort to Ged? He lay that night among corded rolls of pelts from the northern isles and watched the stars of spring above the harbor waters and the little yellow lights of the City astern, and he slept and waked again full of delight. Before dawn the tide turned. They raised anchor and rowed softly out between the Armed Cliffs. As sunrise reddened the Mountain of Gont behind them they raised the high sail and ran southwestward over the Gontish Sea.

Between Barnisk and Torheven they sailed with a light wind, and on the second day came in sight of Havnor, the Great Island, heart and hearth of the Archipelago. For three days they were in sight of the green hills of Havnor as they worked along its eastern coast, but they did not come to shore. Not for many years did Ged set foot on that land or see the white towers of Havnor Great Port at the center of the world.

They lay over one night at Kembermouth, the northern port of Way Island, and the next at a little town on the entrance of Felkway Bay, and the next day passed the northern cape of O and entered the Ebavnor Straits. There they dropped sail and rowed, always with land on either side and always within hail of other ships, great and small, merchants and traders, some bound in from the Outer Reaches with strange cargo after a voyage of years and others that hopped like sparrows from isle to isle of the Inmost Sea. Turning southward out of the crowded Straits they left Havnor astern and sailed between the two fair islands Ark and Ilien, towered and terraced with cities, and then through rain and rising wind began to beat their way across the Inmost Sea to Roke Island.

In the night as the wind freshened to a gale they took down both sail and mast, and the next day, all day, they rowed. The long ship lay steady on the waves and went gallantly, but the steersman at the long steering-sweep in the stern looked into the rain that beat the sea and saw nothing but the rain. They went southwest by the pointing of the magnet, knowing how they went, but not through

what waters. Ged heard men speak of the shoal
waters north of Roke, and of the Borilous Rocks
to the east; others argued that they might be far
out of course by now, in the empty waters south of
Kamery. Still the wind grew stronger, tearing the
edges of the great waves into flying tatters of foam,
and still they rowed southwest with the wind behind them. The stints at the oars were shortened,
for the labor was very hard; the younger lads were
set two to an oar, and Ged took his turn with the
others as he had since they left Gont. When they
did not row they bailed, for the seas broke heavy
on the ship. So they labored among the waves that
ran like smoking mountains under the wind, while
the rain beat hard and cold on their backs, and the
drum thumped through the noise of the storm like
a heart thumping.

A man came to take Ged's place at the oar, sending him to the ship's master in the bow. Rainwater
dripped from the hem of the master's cloak, but
he stood stout as a winebarrel on his bit of deck-
ing and looking down at Ged he asked, "Can you
abate this wind, lad?"

"No, sir."

"Have you craft with iron?"

He meant, could Ged make the compass-needle
point their way to Roke, making the magnet follow

not its north but their need. That skill is a secret of the Seamasters, and again Ged must say no.

"Well then," the master bellowed through the wind and rain, "you must find some ship to take you back to Roke from Hort Town. Roke must be west of us now, and only wizardry could bring us there through this sea. We must keep south."

Ged did not like this, for he had heard the sailors talk of Hort Town, how it was a lawless place, full of evil traffic, where men were often taken and sold into slavery in the South Reach. Returning to his labor at the oar he pulled away with his companion, a sturdy Andradean lad, and heard the drum beat the stroke and saw the lantern hung on the stern bob and flicker as the wind plucked it about, a tormented fleck of light in the rain-lashed dusk. He kept looking to westward, as often as he could in the heavy rhythm of pulling the oar. And as the ship rose on a high swell he saw for a moment over the dark smoking water a light between clouds, as it might be the last gleam of sunset: but this was a clear light, not red.

His oar-mate had not seen it, but he called it out. The steersman watched for it on each rise of the great waves, and saw it as Ged saw it again, but shouted back that it was only the setting sun. Then Ged called to one of the lads that was bailing to take his place on the bench a minute, and made his way forward again along the encumbered aisle between the benches, and catching hold of the carved prow to keep from being pitched overboard he shouted up to the master, "Sir! that light to the west is Roke Island!"

"I saw no light," the master roared, but even as he spoke Ged flung out his arm pointing, and all saw the light gleam clear in the west over the heaving scud and tumult of the sea.

Not for his passenger's sake, but to save his ship from the peril of the storm, the master shouted at once to the steersman to head westward toward the light. But he said to Ged, "Boy, you speak like a Seamaster, but I tell you if you lead us wrong in this weather I will throw you over to swim to Roke!"

Now instead of running before the storm they must row across the wind's way, and it was hard: waves striking the ship abeam pushed her always south of their new course, and rolled her, and filled her with water so that bailing must be ceaseless, and the oarsmen must watch lest the ship rolling should lift their oars out of water as they pulled and so pitch them down among the benches. It was nearly dark under the stormclouds, but now and again they made out the light to the west, enough to set course by, and so struggled on. At last the wind dropped a little, and the light grew broad before them. They rowed on, and they came as it were through a curtain, between one oarstroke and the next running out of the storm into a clear air, where the light of after-sunset glowed in the sky and on the sea. Over the foamcrested waves they saw not far off a high, round, green hill, and beneath it a town built on a small bay where boats lay at anchor, all in peace.

The steersman leaning on his long sweep turned his head and called, "Sir! is this true land or a witchery?"

"Keep her as she goes, you witless woodenhead! Row, you spineless slave-sons! That's Thwil Bay and the Knoll of Roke, as any fool could see! Row!"

So to the beat of the drum they rowed wearily into the bay. There it was still, so that they could hear the voices of people up in the town, and a bell ringing, and only far off the hiss and roaring of the storm. Clouds hung dark to north and east and south a mile off all about the island. But over Roke stars were coming out one by one in a clear and quiet sky.

# CHAPTER 3

# THE SCHOOL FOR WIZARDS

GED SLEPT THAT NIGHT ABOARD *Shadow,* and early in the morning parted with those first sea-comrades of his, they shouting good wishes cheerily after him as he went up the docks. The town of Thwil is not large, its high houses huddling close over a few steep narrow streets. To Ged, however, it seemed a city, and not knowing where to go he asked the first townsman of Thwil he met where he would find the Warder of the School on Roke. The man looked at him sidelong a while and said, "The wise don't need to ask, the fool asks in vain," and so went on along the street. Ged went uphill till he came out into a square, rimmed on three sides by the houses with their sharp slate roofs and on the fourth side by the wall of a great building whose few small windows were higher than the chimney-tops of the houses: a fort or castle it seemed, built of mighty grey blocks of stone. In the square beneath it market-booths were set up and there was some coming and going of people. Ged asked his question of an old woman with a basket of mussels, and she replied, "You cannot always find the Warder where he is, but sometimes you find him where he is not," and went on crying her mussels to sell.

In the great building, near one corner, there was a mean little door of wood. Ged went to this and knocked loud. To the old man who opened the door he said, "I bear a letter from the Mage Ogion of Gont to the Warder of the School on this island. I want to find the Warder, but I will not hear more riddles and scoffing!"

"This is the School," the old man said mildy. "I am the doorkeeper. Enter if you can."

Ged stepped forward. It seemed to him that he had passed through the doorway: yet he stood outside on the pavement where he had stood before.

Once more he stepped forward, and once more he remained standing outside the door. The doorkeeper, inside, watched him with mild eyes.

Ged was not so much baffled as angry, for this seemed like a further mockery to him. With voice and hand he made the Opening spell which his aunt had taught him long ago; it was the prize among all her stock of spells, and he wove it well now. But it was only a witch's charm, and the power that held this doorway was not moved at all.

When that failed Ged stood a long while there on the pavement. At last he looked at the old man

who waited inside. "I cannot enter," he said unwill-
ingly, "unless you help me."

The doorkeeper answered, "Say your name."

Then again Ged stood still a while; for a man
never speaks his own name aloud, until more than
his life's safety is at stake.

"I am Ged," he said aloud. Stepping forward
then he entered the open doorway. Yet it seemed
to him that though the light was behind him, a
shadow followed him in at his heels.

He saw also as he turned that the doorway
through which he had come was not plain wood as
he had thought, but ivory without joint or seam: it
was cut, as he knew later, from a tooth of the Great
Dragon. The door that the old man closed behind
him was of polished horn, through which the daylight shone dimly, and on its inner face was carved
the Thousand-Leaved Tree.

"Welcome to this house, lad," the doorkeeper
said, and without saying more led him through
halls and corridors to an open court far inside the
walls of the building. The court was partly paved
with stone, but was roofless, and on a grassplot a
fountain played under young trees in the sunlight.
There Ged waited alone some while. He stood still,
and his heart beat hard, for it seemed to him that
he felt presences and powers at work unseen about
him here, and he knew that this place was built not

only of stone but of magic stronger than stone. He stood in the innermost room of the House of the Wise, and it was open to the sky. Then suddenly he was aware of a man clothed in white who watched him through the falling water of the fountain.

As their eyes met, a bird sang aloud in the branches of the tree. In that moment Ged understood the singing of the bird, and the language of the water falling in the basin of the fountain, and the shape of the clouds, and the beginning and end of the wind that stirred the leaves: it seemed to him that he himself was a word spoken by the sunlight.

Then that moment passed, and he and the world were as before, or almost as before. He went forward to kneel before the Archmage, holding out to him the letter written by Ogion.

The Archmage Nemmerle, Warder of Roke, was an old man, older it was said than any man then living. His voice quavered like the bird's voice when he spoke, welcoming Ged kindly. His hair and beard and robe were white, and he seemed as if all darkness and heaviness had been leached out of him by the slow usage of the years, leaving him white and worn as driftwood that has been a century adrift. "My eyes are old, I cannot read what your master writes," he said in his quavering voice. "Read me the letter, lad."

So Ged made out and read aloud the writing,

which was in Hardic runes, and said no more than
this: *Lord Nemmerle! I send you one who will be
greatest of the wizards of Gont, if the wind blow true.*
This was signed, not with Ogion's true name which
Ged had never yet learned, but with Ogion's rune,
the Closed Mouth.

"He who holds the earthquake on a leash has
sent you, for which be doubly welcome. Young
Ogion was dear to me, when he came here from
Gont. Now tell me of the seas and portents of your
voyage, lad."

"A fair passage, Lord, but for the storm yesterday."

"What ship brought you here?"

"*Shadow*, trading from the Andrades."

"Whose will sent you here?"

"My own."

The Archmage looked at Ged and looked away,
and began to speak in a tongue that Ged did not understand, mumbling as will an old old man whose
wits go wandering among the years and islands. Yet
in among his mumbling there were words of what
the bird had sung and what the water had said falling. He was not laying a spell and yet there was a
power in his voice that moved Ged's mind so that
the boy was bewildered, and for an instant seemed
to behold himself standing in a strange vast desert
place alone among shadows. Yet all along he was in
the sunlit court, hearing the fountain fall.

A great black bird, a raven of Osskil, came walking over the stone terrace and the grass. It came to the hem of the Archmage's robe and stood there all black with its dagger beak and eyes like pebbles, staring sidelong at Ged. It pecked three times on the white staff Nemmerle leaned on, and the old wizard ceased his muttering, and smiled. "Run and play, lad," he said at last as to a little child. Ged knelt again on one knee to him. When he rose, the Archmage was gone. Only the raven stood eyeing him, its beak outstretched as if to peck the vanished staff.

It spoke, in what Ged guessed might be the speech of Osskil. "Terrenon ussbuk!" it said croaking. "Terrenon ussbuk orrek!" And it strutted off as it had come.

Ged turned to leave the courtyard, wondering where he should go. Under the archway he was met by a tall youth who greeted him very courteously, bowing his head. "I am called Jasper, Enwit's son of the Domain of Eolg on Havnor Isle. I am at your service today, to show you about the Great House and answer your questions as I can. How shall I call you, Sir?"

Now it seemed to Ged, a mountain villager who had never been among the sons of rich merchants and noblemen, that this fellow was scoffing at him with his "service" and his "Sir" and his bowing and scraping. He answered shortly, "Sparrowhawk, they call me."

The other waited a moment as if expecting some more mannerly response, and getting none straightened up and turned a little aside. He was two or three years older than Ged, very tall, and he moved and carried himself with stiff grace, posing (Ged thought) like a dancer. He wore a grey cloak with hood thrown back. The first place he took Ged was the wardrobe room, where as a student of the school Ged might find himself another such cloak that fitted him, and any other clothing he might need. He put on the dark-grey cloak he had chosen, and Jasper said, "Now you are one of us."

Jasper had a way of smiling faintly as he spoke which made Ged look for a jeer hidden in his polite words. "Do clothes make the mage?" he answered, sullen.

"No," said the older boy. "Though I have heard that manners make the man . . . Where now?"

"Where you will. I do not know the house."

Jasper took him down the corridors of the Great House showing him the open courts and the roofed halls, the Room of Shelves where the books of lore and rune-tomes were kept, the great Hearth Hall where all the school gathered on festival days, and upstairs, in the towers and under the roofs, the small cells where the students and Masters slept.

Ged's was in the South Tower, with a window looking down over the steep roofs of Thwil town to the sea. Like the other sleeping-cells it had no furnishing but a straw-filled mattress in the corner. "We live very plain here," said Jasper. "But I expect you won't mind that."

"I'm used to it." Presently, trying to show himself an equal of this polite disdainful youth, he added, "I suppose you weren't, when you first came."

Jasper looked at him, and his look said without words, "What could you possibly know about what I, son of the Lord of the Domain of Eolg on the Isle of Havnor, am or am not used to?" What Jasper said aloud was simply, "Come on this way."

A gong had been rung while they were upstairs, and they came down to eat the noon meal at the Long Table of the refectory, along with a hundred or more boys and young men. Each waited on himself, joking with the cooks through the window-hatches of the kitchen that opened into the refectory, loading his plate from great bowls of food that steamed on the sills, sitting where he pleased at the Long Table. "They say," Jasper told Ged, "that no matter how many sit at this table, there is always room." Certainly there was room both for many noisy groups of boys talking and eating mightily, and for older fellows, their grey cloaks clasped with silver at the neck, who sat more quietly by pairs or

alone, with grave, pondering faces, as if they had
much to think about. Jasper took Ged to sit with
a heavyset fellow called Vetch, who said nothing
much but shoveled in his food with a will. He had
the accent of the East Reach, and was very dark
of skin, not red-brown like Ged and Jasper and
most folk of the Archipelago, but black-brown. He
was plain, and his manners were not polished. He
grumbled about the dinner when he had finished
it, but then turning to Ged said, "At least it's not
illusion, like so much around here; it sticks to your
ribs." Ged did not know what he meant, but he felt
a certain liking for him, and was glad when after
the meal he stayed with them.

They went down into the town, that Ged might
learn his way about it. Few and short as were the
streets of Thwil, they turned and twisted curiously
among the high-roofed houses, and the way was
easy to lose. It was a strange town, and strange
also its people, fishermen and workmen and ar-
tisans like any others, but so used to the sorcery
that is ever at play on the Isle of the Wise that they
seemed half sorcerers themselves. They talked (as
Ged had learned) in riddles, and not one of them
would blink to see a boy turn into a fish or a house
fly up into the air, but knowing it for a schoolboy
prank would go on cobbling shoes or cutting up
mutton, unconcerned.

Coming up past the Back Door and around through the gardens of the Great House, the three boys crossed the clear-running Thwilburn on a wooden bridge and went on northward among woods and pastures. The path climbed and wound. They passed oak-groves where shadows lay thick for all the brightness of the sun. There was one grove not far away to the left that Ged could never quite see plainly. The path never reached it, though it always seemed to be about to. He could not even make out what kind of trees they were. Vetch, seeing him gazing, said softly, "That is the Immanent Grove. We can't come there, yet . . ."

In the hot sunlit pastures yellow flowers bloomed. "Sparkweed," said Jasper. "They grow where the wind dropped the ashes of burning Ilien, when Erreth-Akbe defended the Inward Isles from the Firelord." He blew on a withered flowerhead, and the seeds shaken loose went up on the wind like sparks of fire in the sun.

The path led them up and around the base of a great green hill, round and treeless, the hill that Ged had seen from the ship as they entered the charmed waters of Roke Island. On the hillside Jasper halted. "At home in Havnor I heard much about Gontish wizardry, and always in praise, so that I've wanted for a long time to see the manner of it. Here now we have a Gontishman; and we stand on the slopes of Roke Knoll, whose roots go down to the center of the earth. All spells are strong here. Play us a trick, Sparrowhawk. Show us your style."

Ged, confused and taken aback, said nothing.

"Later on, Jasper," Vetch said in his plain way. "Let him be a while."

"He has either skill or power, or the doorkeeper wouldn't have let him in. Why shouldn't he show it, now as well as later? Right, Sparrowhawk?"

"I have both skill and power," Ged said. "Show me what kind of thing you're talking about."

"Illusions, of course—tricks, games of seeming. Like this!"

Pointing his finger Jasper spoke a few strange words, and where he pointed on the hillside among the green grasses a little thread of water trickled, and grew, and now a spring gushed out and the water went running down the hill. Ged put his hand in the stream and it felt wet, drank of it and it was cool. Yet for all that it would quench no thirst, being but illusion. Jasper with another word stopped the water, and the grasses waved dry in the sunlight. "Now you, Vetch," he said with his cool smile.

Vetch scratched his head and looked glum, but he took up a bit of earth in his hand and began to sing tunelessly over it, molding it with his dark fingers and shaping it, pressing it, stroking it: and suddenly it was a small creature like a bumble-bee or furry fly, that flew humming off over Roke Knoll, and vanished.

Ged stood staring, crestfallen. What did he know but mere village witchery, spells to call goats, cure warts, move loads or mend pots?

"I do no such tricks as these," he said. That was enough for Vetch, who was for going on; but Jasper said, "Why don't you?"

"Sorcery is not a game. We Gontishmen do not play it for pleasure or praise," Ged answered haughtily.

"What do you play it for," Jasper inquired, "—money?"

"No!—" But he could not think of anything more to say that would hide his ignorance and save his pride. Jasper laughed, not ill-humoredly, and went on, leading them on around Roke Knoll. And Ged followed, sullen and sore-hearted, knowing he had behaved like a fool, and blaming Jasper for it.

That night as he lay wrapped in his cloak on the mattress in his cold unlit cell of stone, in the utter silence of the Great House of Roke, the strangeness of the place and the thought of all the spells and sorceries that had been worked there began to come over him heavily. Darkness surrounded him, dread filled him. He wished he were anywhere else but Roke. But Vetch came to the door, a little

bluish ball of werelight nodding over his head to
light the way, and asked if he could come in and
talk a while. He asked Ged about Gont, and then
spoke fondly of his own home isles of the East
Reach, telling how the smoke of village hearthfires
is blown across that quiet sea at evening between
the small islands with funny names: Korp, Kopp,
and Holp, Venway and Vemish, Iffish, Koppish,
and Sneg. When he sketched the shapes of those
lands on the stones of the floor with his finger to
show Ged how they lay, the lines he drew shone
dim as if drawn with a stick of silver for a while
before they faded. Vetch had been three years at
the School, and soon would be made sorcerer; he
thought no more of performing the lesser arts of
magic than a bird thinks of flying. Yet a greater,
unlearned skill he possessed, which was the art of
kindness. That night, and always from then on, he
offered and gave Ged friendship, a sure and open
friendship which Ged could not help but return.

Yet Vetch was also friendly to Jasper, who had
made Ged into a fool that first day on Roke Knoll.
Ged would not forget this, nor, it seemed, would
Jasper, who always spoke to him with a polite voice
and a mocking smile. Ged's pride would not be
slighted or condescended to. He swore to prove to
Jasper, and to all the rest of them among whom Jas-

per was something of a leader, how great his power really was—someday. For none of them, for all their clever tricks, had saved a village by wizardry. Of none of them had Ogion written that he would be the greatest wizard of Gont.

So bolstering up his pride, he set all his strong will on the work they gave him, the lessons and crafts and histories and skills taught by the grey-cloaked Masters of Roke, who were called the Nine. Part of each day he studied with the Master Chanter, learning the Deeds of heroes and the Lays of wisdom, beginning with the oldest of all songs, *The Creation of Éa.* Then with a dozen other lads he would practice with the Master Windkey at arts of wind and weather. Whole bright days of spring and early summer they spent out in Roke Bay in light catboats, practicing steering by word, and stilling waves, and speaking to the world's wind, and raising up the magewind. These are very intricate skills, and frequently Ged's head got whacked by the swinging boom as the boat jibed under a wind suddenly blowing backwards, or his boat and another collided though they had the whole bay to navigate in, or all three boys in his boat went swimming unexpectedly as the boat was swamped by a huge, unintended wave. There were quieter expeditions ashore, other days, with the Master Herbal

who taught the ways and properties of things that
grow; and the Master Hand taught sleight and jug-
glery and the lesser arts of Changing.

At all these studies Ged was apt, and within a
month was bettering lads who had been a year at
Roke before him. Especially the tricks of illusion
came to him so easily that it seemed he had been
born knowing them and needed only to be re-
minded. The Master Hand was a gentle and light-
hearted old man, who had endless delight in the
wit and beauty of the crafts he taught; Ged soon
felt no awe of him, but asked him for this spell
and that spell, and always the Master smiled and
showed him what he wanted. But one day, having
it in mind to put Jasper to shame at last, Ged said
to the Master Hand in the Court of Seeming, "Sir,
all these charms are much the same; knowing one,
you know them all. And as soon as the spell-weav-
ing ceases, the illusion vanishes. Now if I make a
pebble into a diamond"—and he did so with a
word and a flick of his wrist—"what must I do to
make that diamond remain diamond? How is the
changing-spell locked, and made to last?"

The Master Hand looked at the jewel that glittered on Ged's palm, bright as the prize of a dragon's hoard. The old Master murmured one word,
"*Tolk*," and there lay the pebble, no jewel but a
rough grey bit of rock. The Master took it and held

it out on his own hand. "This is a rock; *tolk* in the True Speech," he said, looking mildly up at Ged now. "A bit of the stone of which Roke Isle is made, a little bit of the dry land on which men live. It is itself. It is part of the world. By the Illusion-Change you can make it look like a diamond—or a flower or a fly or an eye or a flame—" The rock flickered from shape to shape as he named them, and returned to rock. "But that is mere seeming. Illusion fools the beholder's senses; it makes him see and hear and feel that the thing is changed. But it does not change the thing. To change this rock into a jewel, you must change its true name. And to do that, my son, even to so small a scrap of the world, is to change the world. It can be done. Indeed it can be done. It *is* the art of the Master Changer, and you will learn it, when you are ready to learn it. But you must not change one thing, one pebble, one grain of sand, until you know what good and evil will follow on that act. The world is in balance, in Equilibrium. A wizard's power of Changing and of Summoning can shake the balance of the world. It is dangerous, that power. It is most perilous. It must follow knowledge, and serve need. To light a candle is to cast a shadow . . ."

He looked down at the pebble again. "A rock is a good thing, too, you know," he said, speaking less gravely. "If the Isles of Earthsea were all made of diamond, we'd lead a hard life here. Enjoy illusions, lad, and let the rocks be rocks." He smiled, but Ged left dissatisfied. Press a mage for his secrets and he would always talk, like Ogion, about balance, and danger, and the dark. But surely a wizard, one who had gone past these childish tricks of illusion to the true arts of Summoning and Change, was powerful enough to do what he pleased, and balance the world as seemed best to him, and drive back darkness with his own light.

In the corridor he met Jasper, who, since Ged's accomplishments began to be praised about the School, spoke to him in a way that seemed more friendly, but was more scoffing. "You look gloomy, Sparrowhawk," he said now, "did your juggling-charms go wrong?"

Seeking as always to put himself on equal footing with Jasper, Ged answered the question ignoring its ironic tone. "I'm sick of juggling," he said, "sick of these illusion-tricks, fit only to amuse idle lords in their castles and Domains. The only true magic they've taught me yet on Roke is making werelight, and some weatherworking. The rest is mere foolery."

"Even foolery is dangerous," said Jasper, "in the hands of a fool."

At that Ged turned as if he had been slapped, and took a step towards Jasper; but the older boy smiled as if he had not intended any insult, nodded his head in his stiff, graceful way, and went on.

Standing there with rage in his heart, looking after Jasper, Ged swore to himself to outdo his rival, and not in some mere illusion-match but in a test of power. He would prove himself, and humiliate Jasper. He would not let the fellow stand there looking down at him, graceful, disdainful, hateful.

Ged did not stop to think why Jasper might hate him. He only knew why he hated Jasper. The other prentices had soon learned they could seldom match themselves against Ged either in sport or in earnest, and they said of him, some in praise and some in spite, "He's a wizard born, he'll never let you beat him." Jasper alone neither praised him nor avoided him, but simply looked down at him, smiling slightly. And therefore Jasper stood alone as his rival, who must be put to shame.

He did not see, or would not see, that in this rivalry, which he clung to and fostered as part of his own pride, there was anything of the danger, the darkness, of which the Master Hand had mildly warned him.

When he was not moved by pure rage, he knew very well that he was as yet no match for Jasper, or any of the older boys, and so he kept at his work and went on as usual. At the end of summer the work was slackened somewhat, so there was more time for sport: spell-boat races down in the harbor, feats of illusion in the courts of the Great House, and in the long evenings, in the groves, wild games of hide-and-seek where hiders and seeker were both invisible and only voices moved laughing and calling among the trees, following and dodging the quick, faint werelights. Then as autumn came they set to their tasks afresh, practicing new magic. So Ged's first months at Roke went by fast, full of passions and wonders.

In winter it was different. He was sent with seven other boys across Roke Island to the farthest north-most cape, where stands the Isolate Tower. There by himself lived the Master Namer, who was called by a name that had no meaning in any language, Kurremkarmerruk. No farm or dwelling lay within miles of the Tower. Grim it stood above the northern cliffs, grey were the clouds over the seas of winter, endless the lists and ranks and rounds of names that the Namer's eight pupils must learn. Amongst them in the Tower's high room Kurremkarmerruk sat on a high seat, writing down lists of names that must be learned before the ink faded at midnight leaving the parchment blank again. It was cold and half-dark and always silent there except for the scratching of the Master's pen and the sighing, maybe, of a student who must learn before midnight the name of every cape, point, bay, sound,

inlet, channel, harbor, shallows, reef and rock of
the shores of Lossow, a little islet of the Pelnish Sea.
If the student complained the Master might say
nothing, but lengthen the list; or he might say, "He
who would be Seamaster must know the true name
of every drop of water in the sea."

Ged sighed sometimes, but he did not complain.
He saw that in this dusty and fathomless matter of
learning the true name of every place, thing, and
being, the power he wanted lay like a jewel at the
bottom of a dry well. For magic consists in this, the
true naming of a thing. So Kurremkarmerruk had
said to them, once, their first night in the Tower;
he never repeated it, but Ged did not forget his
words. "Many a mage of great power," he had said,
"has spent his whole life to find out the name of
one single thing—one single lost or hidden name.
And still the lists are not finished. Nor will they
be, till world's end. Listen, and you will see why.
In the world under the sun, and in the other world
that has no sun, there is much that has nothing to
do with men and men's speech, and there are powers beyond our power. But magic, true magic, is
worked only by those beings who speak the Hardic
tongue of Earthsea, or the Old Speech from which
it grew.

"That is the language dragons speak, and the
language Segoy spoke who made the islands of

the world, and the language of our lays and songs, spells, enchantments, and invocations. Its words lie hidden and changed among our Hardic words. We call the foam on waves *sukien:* that word is made from two words of the Old Speech, *suk,* feather, and *inien,* the sea. Feather of the sea is foam. But you cannot charm the foam calling it *sukien;* you must use its own true name in the Old Speech, which is *essa.* Any witch knows a few of these words in the Old Speech, and a mage knows many. But there are many more, and some have been lost over the ages, and some have been hidden, and some are known only to dragons and to the Old Powers of Earth, and some are known to no living creature; and no man could learn them all. For there is no end to that language.

"Here is the reason. The sea's name is *inien,* well and good. But what we call the Inmost Sea has its own name also in the Old Speech. Since no thing can have two true names, *inien* can mean only 'all the sea except the Inmost Sea.' And of course it does not mean even that, for there are seas and bays and straits beyond counting that bear names of their own. So if some Mage-Seamaster were mad enough to try to lay a spell of storm or calm over all the ocean, his spell must say not only that word *inien,* but the name of every stretch and bit and part of the sea through all the Archipelago and all the

Outer Reaches and beyond to where names cease. Thus, that which gives us the power to work magic sets the limits of that power. A mage can control only what is near him, what he can name exactly and wholly. And this is well. If it were not so, the wickedness of the powerful or the folly of the wise would long ago have sought to change what cannot be changed, and Equilibrium would fail. The unbalanced sea would overwhelm the islands where we perilously dwell, and in the old silence all voices and all names would be lost."

Ged thought long on these words, and they went deep in his understanding. Yet the majesty of the task could not make the work of that long year in the Tower less hard and dry; and at the end of the year Kurremkarmerruk said to him, "You have made a good beginning." But no more. Wizards speak truth, and it was true that all the mastery of Names that Ged had toiled to win that year was the mere start of what he must go on learning all his life. He was let go from the Isolate Tower sooner than those who had come with him, for he had learned quicker; but that was all the praise he got.

He walked south across the island alone in the early winter, along townless empty roads. As night came on it rained. He said no charm to keep the rain off him, for the weather of Roke was in the hands of the Master Windkey and might not be tampered with. He took shelter under a great pendick-tree, and lying there wrapped in his cloak he thought of his old master Ogion, who might still be on his autumn wanderings over the heights of Gont, sleeping out with leafless branches for a roof and falling rain for housewalls. That made Ged smile, for he found the thought of Ogion always a comfort to him. He fell asleep with a peaceful heart, there in the cold darkness full of the whisper of water. At dawn waking he lifted his head; the rain had ceased; he saw, sheltered in the folds of his cloak, a little animal curled up asleep which had crept there for warmth. He wondered, seeing it, for it was a rare strange beast, an otak.

These creatures are found only on four southern isles of the Archipelago, Roke, Ensmer, Pody and Wathort. They are small and sleek, with broad faces, and fur dark brown or brindle, and great bright eyes. Their teeth are cruel and their temper fierce, so they are not made pets of. They have no call or cry or any voice. Ged stroked this one, and it woke and yawned, showing a small brown tongue and white teeth, but it was not afraid. "Otak," he said, and then remembering the thousand names of beasts he had learned in the Tower he called it by its true name in the Old Speech, "Hoeg! Do you want to come with me?"

The otak sat itself down on his open hand, and began to wash its fur.

He put it up on his shoulder in the folds of his hood, and there it rode. Sometimes during the day it jumped down and darted off into the woods, but it always came back to him, once with a wood-mouse it had caught. He laughed and told it to eat the mouse, for he was fasting, this night being the Festival of Sunreturn. So he came in the wet dusk past Roke Knoll, and saw bright werelights playing in the rain over the roofs of the Great House, and he entered there and was welcomed by his Masters and companions in the firelit hall.

It was like a homecoming to Ged, who had no home to which he could ever return. He was happy to see so many faces he knew, and happiest to see Vetch come forward to greet him with a wide smile on his dark face. He had missed his friend this year more than he knew. Vetch had been made sorcerer this fall and was a prentice no more, but that set no barrier between them. They fell to talking at once, and it seemed to Ged that he said more to Vetch in that first hour than he had said during the whole long year at the Isolate Tower.

The otak still rode his shoulder, nestling in the fold of his hood as they sat at dinner at long tables set up for the festival in the Hearth Hall. Vetch marveled at the little creature, and once put up his hand to stroke it, but the otak snapped its sharp teeth at him. He laughed. "They say, Sparrowhawk, that a man favored by a wild beast is a man to whom the Old Powers of stone and spring will speak in human voice."

"They say Gontish wizards often keep familiars," said Jasper, who sat on the other side of Vetch. "Our Lord Nemmerle has his raven, and songs say the Red Mage of Ark led a wild boar on a gold chain. But I never heard of any sorcerer keeping a rat in his hood!"

At that they all laughed, and Ged laughed with them. It was a merry night and he was joyful to be there in the warmth and merriment, keeping festival with his companions. But, like all Jasper ever said to him, the jest set his teeth on edge.

That night the Lord of O was a guest of the school, himself a sorcerer of renown. He had been a pupil of the Archmage, and returned sometimes to Roke for the Winter Festival or the Long Dance in summer. With him was his lady, slender and young, bright as new copper, her black hair crowned with opals. It was seldom that any woman sat in the halls of the Great House, and some of the old Masters looked at her sidelong, disapproving. But the young men looked at her with all their eyes.

"For such a one," said Vetch to Ged, "I could

work vast enchantments . . ." He sighed, and laughed.

"She's only a woman," Ged replied.

"The Princess Elfarran was only a woman," said Vetch, "and for her sake all Enlad was laid waste, and the Hero-Mage of Havnor died, and the island Soléa sank beneath the sea."

"Old tales," says Ged. But then he too began to look at the Lady of O, wondering if indeed this was such mortal beauty as the old tales told of.

The Master Chanter had sung the *Deed of the Young King*, and all together had sung the Winter Carol. Now when there was a little pause before they all rose from the tables, Jasper got up and went to the table nearest the hearth, where the Archmage and the guests and Masters sat, and he spoke to the Lady of O. Jasper was no longer a boy but a young man, tall and comely, with his cloak clasped at the neck with silver; for he also had been made sorcerer this year, and the silver clasp was the token of it. The lady smiled at what he said and the opals shone in her black hair, radiant. Then, the Masters nodding benign consent, Jasper worked an illusion-charm for her. A white tree he made spring up from the stone floor. Its branches touched the high roofbeams of the hall, and on every twig of every branch a golden apple shone, each a sun, for it was the Year-Tree. A bird flew among the branches suddenly, all white with a tail like a fall of snow, and the golden apples dimming turned to seeds, each one a drop of crystal. These falling from the tree with a sound like rain, all at once there came a sweet fragrance, while the tree, swaying, put forth leaves of rosy fire and white flowers like stars. So the illusion faded. The Lady of O cried out with pleasure, and bent her shining head to the young sorcerer in praise of his mastery. "Come with us, live with us in O-tokne—can he not come, my lord?" she asked, childlike, of her stern husband. But Jasper said only, "When I have learned skills worthy of my Masters here and worthy of your praise, my lady, then I will gladly come, and serve you ever gladly."

So he pleased all there, except Ged. Ged joined his voice to the praises, but not his heart. "I could have done better," he said to himself, in bitter envy; and all the joy of the evening was darkened for him, after that.

CHAPTER 4

# THE LOOSING OF THE SHADOW

THAT SPRING GED SAW LITTLE of either Vetch or Jasper, for they being sorcerers studied now with the Master Patterner in the secrecy of the Immanent Grove, where no prentice might set foot. Ged stayed in the Great House, working with the Masters at all the skills practiced by sorcerers, those who work magic but carry no staff: windbringing, weatherworking, finding and binding, and the arts of spellsmiths and spellwrights, tellers, chanters, healalls and herbalists. At night alone in his sleeping-cell, a little ball of werelight burning above the book in place of lamp or candle, he studied the Further Runes and the Runes of Éa, which are used in the Great Spells. All these crafts came easy to him, and it was rumored among the students that this Master or that had said that the Gontish lad was the quickest student that had ever been at Roke, and tales grew up concerning the otak, which was said to be a disguised spirit who whispered wisdom in Ged's ear, and it was even said that the Archmage's raven had hailed Ged at his arrival as "Archmage to be." Whether or not they believed such stories, and whether or not they liked Ged, most of his companions admired him, and were eager to follow him when the rare wild mood came over him and he joined them to lead their games on the lengthening evenings of spring. But for the most part he was all work and pride and temper, and held himself apart. Among them all, Vetch being absent, he had no friend, and never knew he wanted one.

He was fifteen, very young to learn any of the High Arts of wizard or mage, those who carry the staff; but he was so quick to learn all the arts of illusion that the Master Changer, himself a young man, soon began to teach him apart from the others, and to tell him about the true Spells of Shaping. He explained how, if a thing is really to be changed into another thing, it must be renamed for as long as the spell lasts, and he told how this affects the names and natures of things surrounding the transformed thing. He spoke of the perils of changing, above all when the wizard transforms his own shape and thus is liable to be caught in his own spell. Little by little, drawn on by the boy's sureness of understanding, the young Master began to do more than merely tell him of these mysteries. He taught him first one and then another of the Great Spells of Change, and he gave him the Book of Shaping to study. This he did without knowledge of the Archmage, and unwisely, yet he meant no harm.

Ged worked also with the Master Summoner now, but that Master was a stern man, aged and hardened by the deep and somber wizardry he taught. He dealt with no illusion, only true magic, the summoning of such energies as light, and heat, and the force that draws the magnet, and those forces men perceive as weight, form, color, sound: real powers, drawn from the immense fathomless energies of the universe, which no man's spells or uses could exhaust or unbalance. The weather-worker's and seamaster's calling upon wind and water were crafts already known to his pupils, but it was he who showed them why the true wizard uses such spells only at need, since to summon up such earthly forces is to change the earth of which they are a part. "Rain on Roke may be drouth in Osskil," he said, "and a calm in the East Reach may be storm and ruin in the West, unless you know what you are about."

As for the calling of real things and living people, and the raising up of spirits of the dead, and the in-vocations of the Unseen, those spells which are the height of the Summoner's art and the mage's power, those he scarcely spoke of to them. Once or twice

Ged tried to lead him to talk a little of such mysteries, but the Master was silent, looking at him long and grimly, till Ged grew uneasy and said no more.

Sometimes indeed he was uneasy working even such lesser spells as the Summoner taught him. There were certain runes on certain pages of the Lore-Book that seemed familiar to him, though he did not remember in what book he had ever seen them before. There were certain phrases that must be said in spells of Summoning that he did not like to say. They made him think, for an instant, of shadows in a dark room, of a shut door and shadows reaching out to him from the corner by the door. Hastily he put such thoughts or memories aside and went on. These moments of fear and darkness, he said to himself, were the shadows merely of his ignorance. The more he learned, the less he would have to fear, until finally in his full power as Wizard he needed fear nothing in the world, nothing at all.

In the second month of that summer all the school gathered again at the Great House to celebrate the Moon's Night and the Long Dance, which that year fell together as one festival of two nights, which happens but once in fifty-two years. All the first night, the shortest night of full moon of the year, flutes played out in the fields, and the narrow streets of Thwil were full of drums and torches, and the sound of singing went out over the moonlit waters of Roke Bay. As the sun rose next morning the Chanters of Roke began to sing the long *Deed of Erreth-Akbe*, which tells how the white towers of Havnor were built, and of Erreth-Akbe's journeys from the Old Island, Éa, through all the Archipelago and the Reaches, until at last in the uttermost West Reach on the edge of the Open Sea he met the dragon Orm; and his bones in shattered armor lie among the dragon's bones on the shore of lonely Selidor, but his sword set atop the highest tower of Havnor still burns red in the sunset above the Inmost Sea. When the chant was finished the Long Dance began. Townsfolk and Masters and students and farmers all together, men and women, danced in the warm dust and dusk down all the roads of Roke to the sea-beaches, to the beat of drums and drone of pipes and flutes. Straight out into the sea they danced, under the moon one night past full, and the music was lost in the breakers' sound. As the east grew light they came back up the beaches and the roads, the drums silent and only the flutes playing soft and shrill. So it was done on every island of the Archipelago that night: one dance, one music binding together the sea-divided lands.

When the Long Dance was over most people slept the day away, and gathered again at evening to eat and drink. There was a group of young fellows, prentices and sorcerers, who had brought their supper out from the refectory to hold a private feast in a courtyard of the Great House: Vetch, Jasper, and Ged were there, and six or seven others, and some young lads released briefly from the Isolate Tower, for this festival had brought even Kurremkarmerruk out. They were all eating and laughing and playing such tricks out of pure frolic as might be the marvel of a king's court. One boy had lighted the court with a hundred stars of werelight, colored like jewels, that swung in a slow netted procession between them and the real stars; and a pair of boys were playing bowls with balls of green flame and bowling-pins that leaped and hopped away as the ball came near; and all the while Vetch sat crosslegged, eating roast chicken, up in mid-air. One of the younger boys tried to pull him down to earth, but Vetch merely drifted up a little higher, out of reach, and sat calmly smiling on the air. Now and then he tossed away a chicken bone, which turned to an owl and flew hooting among the netted starlights. Ged shot breadcrumb arrows after the owls and brought them down, and when they touched the ground there they lay, bone and crumb, all illusion gone. Ged also tried to join Vetch up in the middle of the air, but lacking the key of the spell he had to flap his arms to keep aloft, and they were all laughing at his flights and flaps and bumps.

He kept up his foolishness for the laughter's sake, laughing with them, for after those two long nights of dance and moonlight and music and magery he was in a fey and wild mood, ready for whatever might come.

He came lightly down on his feet just beside Jasper at last, and Jasper, who never laughed aloud, moved away saying, "The Sparrowhawk that can't fly . . ."

"Is jasper a precious stone?" Ged returned, grinning. "O Jewel among sorcerers, O Gem of Havnor, sparkle for us!"

The lad that had set the lights dancing sent one down to dance and glitter about Jasper's head. Not quite as cool as usual, frowning, Jasper brushed the light away and snuffed it out with one gesture. "I am sick of boys and noise and foolishness," he said.

"You're getting middle-aged, lad," Vetch remarked from above.

"If silence and gloom is what you want," put in one of the younger boys, "you could always try the Tower."

Ged said to him, "What is it you want, then, Jasper?"

"I want the company of my equals," Jasper said. "Come on, Vetch. Leave the prentices to their toys."

Ged turned to face Jasper. "What do sorcerers have that prentices lack?" he inquired. His voice was quiet, but all the other boys suddenly fell still, for in his tone as in Jasper's the spite between them now sounded plain and clear as steel coming out of a sheath.

"Power," Jasper said.

"I'll match your power act for act."

"You challenge me?"

"I challenge you."

Vetch had dropped down to the ground, and now he came between them, grim of face. "Duels in sorcery are forbidden to us, and well you know it. Let this cease!"

Both Ged and Jasper stood silent, for it was true they knew the law of Roke, and they also knew that Vetch was moved by love, and themselves by hate. Yet their anger was balked, not cooled. Presently, moving a little aside as if to be heard by Vetch alone, Jasper spoke, with his cool smile: "I think you'd better remind your goatherd friend again of the law that protects him. He looks sulky. I wonder, did he really think I'd accept a challenge from him? a fellow who smells of goats, a prentice who doesn't know the First Change?"

"Jasper," said Ged, "what do you know of what I know?"

For an instant, with no word spoken that any heard, Ged vanished from their sight, and where he had stood a great falcon hovered, opening its hooked beak to scream: for one instant, and then Ged stood again in the flickering torchlight, his dark gaze on Jasper.

Jasper had taken a step backward, in astonishment; but now he shrugged and said one word: "Illusion."

The others muttered. Vetch said, "That was not illusion. It was true change. And enough. Jasper, listen—"

"Enough to prove that he sneaked a look in the Book of Shaping behind the Master's back: what then? Go on, Goatherd. I like this trap you're building for yourself. The more you try to prove yourself my equal, the more you show yourself for what you are."

At that, Vetch turned from Jasper, and said very softly to Ged, "Sparrowhawk, will you be a man and drop this now—come with me—"

Ged looked at his friend and smiled, but all he said was, "Keep Hoeg for me a little while, will you?" He put into Vetch's hands the little otak, which as usual had been riding on his shoulder. It had never let any but Ged touch it, but it came to Vetch now, and climbing up his arm cowered on his shoulder, its great bright eyes always on its master.

"Now," Ged said to Jasper, quietly as before, "what are you going to do to prove yourself my superior, Jasper?"

"I don't have to do anything, Goatherd. Yet I will. I will give you a chance—an opportunity. Envy eats you like a worm in an apple. Let's let out the worm. Once by Roke Knoll you boasted that Gontish wizards don't play games. Come to Roke Knoll now and show us what it is they do instead. And afterward, maybe I will show you a little sorcery."

"Yes, I should like to see that," Ged answered. The younger boys, used to seeing his black temper break out at the least hint of slight or insult, watched him in wonder at his coolness now. Vetch watched him not in wonder, but with growing fear. He tried to intervene again, but Jasper said, "Come, keep out of this, Vetch. What will you do with the chance I give you, Goatherd? Will you show us an illusion, a fireball, a charm to cure goats with the mange?"

"What would you like me to do, Jasper?"

The older lad shrugged, "Summon up a spirit from the dead, for all I care!"

"I will."

"You will not." Jasper looked straight at him, rage suddenly flaming out over his disdain. "You will not. You cannot. You brag and brag—"

"By my name, I will do it!"

They all stood utterly motionless for a moment.

Breaking away from Vetch who would have held him back by main force, Ged strode out of the courtyard, not looking back. The dancing werelights overhead died out, sinking down. Jasper hesitated a second, then followed after Ged. And the rest came straggling behind, in silence, curious and afraid.

THE SLOPES OF ROKE KNOLL went up dark into the darkness of summer night before moonrise. The presence of that hill where many wonders had been worked was heavy, like a weight in the air about them. As they came onto the hillside they thought of how the roots of it were deep, deeper than the sea, reaching down even to the old, blind, secret fires at the world's core. They stopped on the east slope. Stars hung over the black grass above them on the hill's crest. No wind blew.

Ged went a few paces up the slope away from the others and turning said in a clear voice, "Jasper! Whose spirit shall I call?"

"Call whom you like. None will listen to you." Jasper's voice shook a little, with anger perhaps. Ged answered him softly, mockingly, "Are you afraid?"

He did not even listen for Jasper's reply, if he made one. He no longer cared about Jasper. Now that they stood on Roke Knoll, hate and rage were gone, replaced by utter certainty. He need envy no one. He knew that his power, this night, on this dark enchanted ground, was greater than it had ever been, filling him till he trembled with the sense of strength barely kept in check. He knew now that Jasper was far beneath him, had been sent perhaps only to bring him here tonight, no rival but a mere servant of Ged's destiny. Under his feet he felt the hillroots going down and down into the dark, and over his head he saw the dry, far fires of the stars. Between, all things were his to order, to command. He stood at the center of the world.

"Don't be afraid," he said, smiling. "I'll call a woman's spirit. You need not fear a woman. Elfarran I will call, the fair lady of the *Deed of Enlad*."

"She died a thousand years ago, her bones lie afar under the Sea of Éa, and maybe there never was such a woman."

"Do years and distances matter to the dead? Do the Songs lie?" Ged said with the same gentle mockery, and then saying, "Watch the air between my hands," he turned away from the others and stood still.

In a great slow gesture he stretched out his arms,

the gesture of welcome that opens an invocation.
He began to speak.

He had read the runes of this Spell of Summoning in Ogion's book, two years and more ago, and
never since had seen them. In darkness he had read
them then. Now in this darkness it was as if he
read them again on the page open before him in
the night. But now he understood what he read,
speaking it aloud word after word, and he saw the
markings of how the spell must be woven with the
sound of the voice and the motion of body and
hand.

The other boys stood watching, not speaking,
not moving unless they shivered a little: for the
great spell was beginning to work. Ged's voice was
soft still, but changed, with a deep singing in it,
and the words he spoke were not known to them.
He fell silent. Suddenly the wind rose roaring in
the grass. Ged dropped to his knees and called out
aloud. Then he fell forward as if to embrace earth
with his outstretched arms, and when he rose he
held something dark in his straining hands and
arms, something so heavy that he shook with effort
getting to his feet. The hot wind whined in the
black tossing grasses on the hill. If the stars shone
now none saw them.

The words of the enchantment hissed and mumbled on Ged's lips, and then he cried out aloud and clearly, "Elfarran!"

Again he cried the name, "Elfarran!"

And the third time, "Elfarran!"

The shapeless mass of darkness he had lifted split apart. It sundered, and a pale spindle of light gleamed between his opened arms, a faint oval reaching from the ground up to the height of his raised hands. In the oval of light for a moment there moved a form, a human shape: a tall woman looking back over her shoulder. Her face was beautiful, and sorrowful, and full of fear.

Only for a moment did the spirit glimmer there. Then the sallow oval between Ged's arms grew bright. It widened and spread, a rent in the darkness of the earth and night, a ripping open of the fabric of the world. Through it blazed a terrible brightness. And through that bright misshapen breach clambered something like a clot of black shadow, quick and hideous, and it leaped straight out at Ged's face.

Staggering back under the weight of the thing, Ged gave a short, hoarse scream. The little otak watching from Vetch's shoulder, the animal that had no voice, screamed aloud also and leaped as if to attack.

Ged fell, struggling and writhing, while the bright rip in the world's darkness above him widened and stretched. The boys that watched fled, and Jasper bent down to the ground hiding his eyes from the terrible light. Vetch alone ran forward to his friend. So only he saw the lump of shadow that clung to Ged, tearing at his flesh. It was like a black beast, the size of a young child, though it seemed to swell and shrink; and it had no head or face, only the four taloned paws with which it gripped and tore. Vetch sobbed with horror, yet he put out his hands to try to pull the thing away from Ged. Before he touched it, he was bound still, unable to move.

The intolerable brightness faded, and slowly the torn edges of the world closed together. Nearby a voice was speaking as softly as a tree whispers or a fountain plays.

Starlight began to shine again, and the grasses of the hillside were whitened with the light of the moon just rising. The night was healed. Restored and steady lay the balance of light and dark. The shadow-beast was gone. Ged lay sprawled on his back, his arms flung out as if they yet kept the wide gesture of welcome and invocation. His face was blackened with blood and there were great black stains on his shirt. The little otak cowered by his shoulder, quivering. And above him stood an old man whose cloak glimmered pale in the moonrise: the Archmage Nemmerle.

The end of Nemmerle's staff hovered silvery above Ged's breast. Once gently it touched him over the heart, once on the lips, while Nemmerle whispered. Ged stirred, and his lips parted gasping for breath. Then the old Archmage lifted the staff, and set it to earth, and leaned heavily on it with bowed head, as if he had scarcely strength to stand.

Vetch found himself free to move. Looking around, he saw that already others were there, the Masters Summoner and Changer. An act of great wizardry is not worked without arousing such men, and they had ways of coming very swiftly when need called, though none had been so swift as the Archmage. They now sent for help, and some who came went with the Archmage, while others, Vetch among them, carried Ged to the chambers of the Master Herbal.

All night long the Summoner stayed on Roke Knoll, keeping watch. Nothing stirred there on the hillside where the stuff of the world had been torn open. No shadow came crawling through moonlight seeking the rent through which it might clamber back into its own domain. It had fled from Nemmerle, and from the mighty spell-walls that surround and protect Roke Island, but it was in the world now. In the world, somewhere, it hid. If Ged had died that night it might have tried to find the doorway he had opened, and follow him into death's realm, or slip back into whatever place it had come from; for this the Summoner waited on Roke Knoll. But Ged lived.

They had laid him abed in the healing-chamber, and the Master Herbal tended the wounds he had on his face and throat and shoulder. They were deep, ragged, and evil wounds. The black blood in them would not stanch, welling out even under the charms and the cobweb-wrapped perriot leaves laid upon them. Ged lay blind and dumb in fever like a stick in a slow fire, and there was no spell to cool what burned him.

Not far away, in the unroofed court where the fountain played, the Archmage lay also unmoving, but cold, very cold: only his eyes lived, watching the fall of moonlit water and the stir of moonlit leaves. Those with him said no spells and worked no healing. Quietly they spoke among themselves from time to time, and then turned again to watch their Lord. He lay still, hawk nose and high forehead and white hair bleached by moonlight all to the color of bone. To check the ungoverned spell and drive off the shadow from Ged, Nemmerle had spent all his power, and with it his bodily strength was gone. He lay dying. But the death of a great mage, who has many times in his life walked on the dry steep hillsides of death's kingdom, is a strange matter: for the dying man goes not blindly, but surely, knowing the way. When Nemmerle looked up through the leaves of the tree, those with him did not know if he watched the stars of summer fading in daybreak, or those other stars, which never set above the hills that see no dawn.

The raven of Osskil that had been his pet for thirty years was gone. No one had seen where it went. "It flies before him," the Master Patterner said, as they kept vigil.

The day came warm and clear. The Great House and the streets of Thwil were hushed. No voice was raised, until along towards noon iron bells spoke out aloud in the Chanter's Tower, harshly tolling.

On the next day the Nine Masters of Roke gathered in a place somewhere under the dark trees of the Immanent Grove. Even there they set nine walls of silence about them, that no person or power might speak to them or hear them as they chose from amongst the mages of all Earthsea him who would be the new Archmage. Gensher of Way was chosen. A ship was sent forth at once across the Inmost Sea to Way Island to bring the Archmage back to Roke. The Master Windkey stood in the stern and raised up the magewind into the sail, and quickly the ship departed, and was gone.

Of these events Ged knew nothing. For four weeks of that hot summer he lay blind, and deaf, and mute, though at times he moaned and cried out like an animal. At last, as the patient crafts of the Master Herbal worked their healing, his wounds began to close and the fever left him. Little by little he seemed to hear again, though he never spoke. On a clear day of autumn the Master Herbal opened the shutters of the room where Ged lay. Since the darkness of that night on Roke Knoll he had known only darkness. Now he saw daylight, and the sun shining. He hid his scarred face in his hands and wept.

Still when winter came he could speak only with a stammering tongue, and the Master Herbal kept him there in the healing-chambers, trying to lead his body and mind gradually back to strength. It was early spring when at last the Master released him, sending him first to offer his fealty to the Archmage Gensher. For he had not been able to join all the others of the School in this duty when Gensher came to Roke.

None of his companions had been allowed to visit him in the months of his sickness, and now as he passed some of them asked one another, "Who is that?" He had been light and lithe and strong. Now, lamed by pain, he went hesitantly, and did not raise his face, the left side of which was white with scars. He avoided those who knew him and

those who did not, and made his way straight to
the court of the Fountain. There where once he
had awaited Nemmerle, Gensher awaited him.

Like the old Archmage the new one was cloaked
in white; but like most men of Way and the East
Reach Gensher was black-skinned, and his look
was black, under thick brows.

Ged knelt and offered him fealty and obedience.
Gensher was silent a while.

"I know what you did," he said at last, "but not
what you are. I cannot accept your fealty."

Ged stood up, and set his hand on the trunk of
the young tree beside the fountain to steady himself. He was still very slow to find words. "Am I to
leave Roke, my lord?"

"Do you want to leave Roke?"

"No."

"What do you want?"

"To stay. To learn. To undo . . . the evil . . ."

"Nemmerle himself could not do that. No, I
would not let you go from Roke. Nothing protects
you but the power of the Masters here and the defenses laid upon this island that keep the creatures
of evil away. If you left now, the thing you loosed
would find you at once, and enter into you, and
possess you. You would be no man but a *gebbeth*,
a puppet doing the will of that evil shadow which
you raised up into the sunlight. You must stay here,

until you gain strength and wisdom enough to defend yourself from it—if ever you do. Even now it waits for you. Assuredly it waits for you. Have you seen it since that night?"

"In dreams, lord." After a while Ged went on, speaking with pain and shame, "Lord Gensher, I do not know what it was—the thing that came out of the spell and cleaved to me—"

"Nor do I know. It has no name. You have great power inborn in you, and you used that power wrongly, to work a spell over which you had no control, not knowing how that spell affects the balance of light and dark, life and death, good and evil. And you were moved to do this by pride and by hate. Is it any wonder the result was ruin? You summoned a spirit from the dead, but with it came one of the Powers of unlife. Uncalled it came from a place where there are no names. Evil, it wills to work evil through you. The power you had to call it gives it power over you: you are connected. It is the shadow of your arrogance, the shadow of your ignorance, the shadow you cast. Has a shadow a name?"

Ged stood sick and haggard. He said at last, "Better I had died."

"Who are you to judge that, you for whom Nemmerle gave his life?—You are safe here. You will live here, and go on with your training. They tell me you were clever. Go on and do your work. Do it well. It is all you can do."

So Gensher ended, and was suddenly gone, as is the way of mages. The fountain leaped in the sunlight, and Ged watched it a while and listened to its voice, thinking of Nemmerle. Once in that court he had felt himself to be a word spoken by the sunlight. Now the darkness also had spoken: a word that could not be unsaid.

He left the court, going to his old room in the South Tower, which they had kept empty for him. He stayed there alone. When the gong called to supper he went, but he would hardly speak to the other lads at the Long Table, or raise his face to them, even those who greeted him most gently. So after a day or two they all left him alone. To be alone was his desire, for he feared the evil he might do or say unwittingly.

Neither Vetch nor Jasper was there, and he did not ask about them. The boys he had led and lorded over were all ahead of him now, because of the months he had lost, and that spring and summer he studied with lads younger than himself. Nor did he shine among them, for the words of any spell, even the simplest illusion-charm, came halting from his tongue, and his hands faltered at their craft.

In autumn he was to go once again to the Isolate Tower to study with the Master Namer. This task which he had once dreaded now pleased him, for silence was what he sought, and long learning where no spells were wrought, and where that power which he knew was still in him would never be called upon to act.

The night before he left for the Tower a visitor came to his room, one wearing a brown traveling-cloak and carrying a staff of oak shod with iron. Ged stood up at sight of the wizard's staff.

"Sparrowhawk—"

At the sound of the voice, Ged raised his eyes: it was Vetch standing there, solid and foursquare as ever, his black blunt face older but his smile unchanged. On his shoulder crouched a little beast, brindle-furred and bright-eyed.

"He stayed with me while you were sick, and now I'm sorry to part with him. And sorrier to part with you, Sparrowhawk. But I'm going home. Here, hoeg! go to your true master!" Vetch patted the otak and set it down on the floor. It went and sat on Ged's pallet, and began to wash its fur with a dry brown tongue like a little leaf. Vetch laughed, but Ged could not smile. He bent down to hide his face, stroking the otak.

"I thought you wouldn't come to me, Vetch," he said.

He did not mean any reproach, but Vetch an-

swered, "I couldn't come to you. The Master Herbal forbade me; and since winter I've been with the
Master in the Grove, locked up myself. I was not
free, until I earned my staff. Listen: when you too
are free, come to the East Reach. I will be waiting
for you. There's good cheer in the little towns there,
and wizards are well received."

"Free . . ." Ged muttered, and shrugged a little,
trying to smile.

Vetch looked at him, not quite as he had used to
look, with no less love but more wizardry, perhaps.
He said gently, "You won't stay bound on Roke
forever."

"Well . . . I have thought, perhaps I may come
to work with the Master in the Tower, to be one of
those who seek among the books and the stars for
lost names, and so . . . so do no more harm, if not
much good . . ."

"Maybe," said Vetch. "I am no seer, but I see
before you, not rooms and books, but far seas, and
the fire of dragons, and the towers of cities, and all
such things a hawk sees when he flies far and high."

"And behind me—what do you see behind me?"
Ged asked, and stood up as he spoke, so that the
werelight that burned overhead between them sent
his shadow back against the wall and floor. Then
he turned his face aside and said, stammering, "But
tell me where you will go, what you will do."

"I will go home, to see my brothers and the sister you have heard me speak of. I left her a little child and soon she'll be having her Naming—it's strange to think of! And so I'll find me a job of wizardry somewhere among the little isles. Oh, I would stay and talk with you, but I can't, my ship goes out tonight and the tide is turned already. Sparrowhawk, if ever your way lies East, come to me. And if ever you need me, send for me, call on me by my name: Estarriol."

At that Ged lifted his scarred face, meeting his friend's eyes.

"Estarriol," he said, "my name is Ged."

Then quietly they bade each other farewell, and Vetch turned and went down the stone hallway, and left Roke.

Ged stood still a while, like one who has received great news, and must enlarge his spirit to receive it. It was a great gift that Vetch had given him, the knowledge of his true name.

No one knows a man's true name but himself and his namer. He may choose at length to tell it to his brother, or his wife, or his friend, yet even those few will never use it where any third person may hear it. In front of other people they will, like other people, call him by his use-name, his nickname—such a name as Sparrowhawk, and Vetch, and Ogion, which means "fircone." If plain men

hide their true name from all but a few they love
and trust utterly, so much more must wizardly
men, being more dangerous, and more endangered.
Who knows a man's name, holds that man's life in
his keeping. Thus to Ged, who had lost faith in
himself, Vetch had given that gift only a friend can
give, the proof of unshaken, unshakable trust.

Ged sat down on his pallet and let the globe
of werelight die, giving off as it faded a faint whiff
of marsh-gas. He petted the otak, which stretched
comfortably and went to sleep on his knee as if it
had never slept anywhere else. The Great House
was silent. It came to Ged's mind that this was the
eve of his own Passage, the day on which Ogion
had given him his name. Four years were gone since
then. He remembered the coldness of the mountain spring through which he had walked naked
and unnamed. He fell to thinking of other bright
pools in the River Ar, where he had used to swim;
and of Ten Alders village under the great slanting
forests of the mountain; of the shadows of morning across the dusty village street, the fire leaping
under bellows-blast in the smith's smelting-pit on
a winter afternoon, the witch's dark fragrant hut
where the air was heavy with smoke and wreath-
ing spells. He had not thought of these things for
a long time. Now they came back to him, on this
night he was seventeen years old. All the years and

places of his brief broken life came within mind's reach and made a whole again. He knew once more, at last, after this long, bitter, wasted time, who he was and where he was.

But where he must go in the years to come, that he could not see; and he feared to see it.

Next morning he set out across the island, the otak riding on his shoulder as it had used to. This time it took him three days, not two, to walk to the Isolate Tower, and he was bone-weary when he came in sight of the Tower above the spitting, hissing seas of the northern cape. Inside, it was dark as he remembered, and cold as he remembered, and Kurremkarmerruk sat on his high seat writing down lists of names. He glanced at Ged and said without welcome, as if Ged had never been away, "Go to bed; tired is stupid. Tomorrow you may open the Book of the Undertakings of the Makers, learning the names therein."

At winter's end he returned to the Great House. He was made sorcerer then, and the Archmage Gensher accepted at that time his fealty. Thenceforth he studied the high arts and enchantments, passing beyond arts of illusion to the works of real magery, learning what he must know to earn his wizard's staff. The trouble he had had in speaking spells wore off over the months, and skill returned into his hands: yet he was never so quick to learn as he had been, having learned a long hard lesson from fear. Yet no ill portents or encounters followed on his working even of the Great Spells of Making and Shaping, which are most perilous. He came to wonder at times if the shadow he had loosed might have grown weak, or fled somehow out of the world, for it came no more into his dreams. But in his heart he knew such hope was folly.

From the Masters and from ancient Lore-Books Ged learned what he could about such beings as this shadow he had loosed; little was there to learn. No such creature was described or spoken of directly. There were at best hints here and there in the old books of things that might be like the shadow-beast. It was not a ghost of human man, nor was it a creature of the Old Powers of Earth, and yet it seemed it might have some link with these. In the *Matter of the Dragons*, which Ged read very closely, there was a tale of an ancient Dragonlord who had come under the sway of one of the Old Powers, a speaking stone that lay in a far northern land. *"At the Stone's command,"* said the book, *"he did speak to raise up a dead spirit out of the realm of the dead, but his wizardry being bent awry by the Stone's will there came with the dead spirit also a thing not summoned, which did devour him out from within and in his shape walked, destroying men."* But the book did not say what the thing was, nor did it tell the end of the tale. And the Masters did not know where such a shadow might come from: from unlife, the Archmage had said; from the wrong side of the world, said the Master Changer; and the Master Summoner said, "I do not know." The Summoner had come often to sit with Ged in his illness. He was grim and grave as ever, but Ged knew now his compassion, and loved him well. "I do not know. I know of the thing only this: that only a great power could have summoned up such a thing, and perhaps only one power—only one voice—your voice. But what in turn that means, I do not know. You will find out. You must find out, or die, and worse than die . . ." He spoke softly and his eyes were somber as he looked at Ged. "You thought, as a boy, that a mage is one who can do anything. So I thought, once. So did we all. And the truth is that as a man's real power grows and his knowledge widens, ever the way he can follow grows narrower: until at last he chooses nothing, but does only and wholly what he *must do* . . ."

The Archmage sent Ged, after his eighteenth birthday, to work with the Master Patterner. What is learned in the Immanent Grove is not much talked about elsewhere. It is said that no spells are worked there, and yet the place itself is an enchantment. Sometimes the trees of that Grove are seen, and sometimes they are not seen, and they are not always in the same place and part of Roke Island. It is said that the trees of the Grove themselves are wise. It is said that the Master Patterner learns his supreme magery there within the Grove, and if ever the trees should die so shall his wisdom die, and in those days the waters will rise and drown the islands of Earthsea which Segoy raised from the deeps in the time before myth, all the lands where men and dragons dwell.

But all this is hearsay; wizards will not speak of it.

The months went by, and at last on a day of spring Ged returned to the Great House, and he had no idea what would be asked of him next. At the door that gives on the path across the fields to Roke Knoll an old man met him, waiting for him in the doorway. At first Ged did not know him, and then putting his mind to it recalled him as the one who had let him into the School on the day of his coming, five years ago.

The old man smiled, greeting him by name, and asked, "Do you know who I am?"

Now Ged had thought before of how it was always said, the Nine Masters of Roke, although he knew only eight: Windkey, Hand, Herbal, Chanter, Changer, Summoner, Namer, Patterner. It seemed that people spoke of the Archmage as the ninth.

Yet when a new Archmage was chosen, nine Masters met to choose him.

"I think you are the Master Doorkeeper," said Ged.

"I am. Ged, you won entrance to Roke by saying your name. Now you may win your freedom of it by saying mine." So said the old man smiling, and waited. Ged stood dumb.

He knew a thousand ways and crafts and means for finding out names of things and of men, of course; such craft was a part of everything he had learned at Roke, for without it there could be little useful magic done. But to find out the name of a Mage and Master was another matter. A mage's name is better hidden than a herring in the sea, better guarded than a dragon's den. A prying charm will be met with a stronger charm, subtle devices will fail, devious inquiries will be deviously thwarted, and force will be turned ruinously back upon itself.

"You keep a narrow door, Master," said Ged at last. "I must sit out in the fields here, I think, and fast till I grow thin enough to slip through."

"As long as you like," said the Doorkeeper, smiling.

So Ged went off a little way and sat down under an alder on the banks of the Thwilburn, letting his otak run down to play in the stream and hunt the muddy banks for creek-crabs. The sun went down, late and bright, for spring was well along. Lights of lantern and werelight gleamed in the windows of the Great House, and down the hill the streets of Thwil town filled with darkness. Owls hooted over the roofs and bats flitted in the dusk air above the stream, and still Ged sat thinking how he might, by force, ruse, or sorcery, learn the Doorkeeper's name. The more he pondered the less he saw, among all the arts of witchcraft he had learned in these five years on Roke, any one that would serve to wrest such a secret from such a mage.

He lay down in the field and slept under the stars, with the otak nestling in his pocket. After the sun was up he went, still fasting, to the door of the House and knocked. The Doorkeeper opened.

"Master," said Ged, "I cannot take your name from you, not being strong enough, and I cannot trick your name from you, not being wise enough. So I am content to stay here, and learn or serve, whatever you will: unless by chance you will answer a question I have."

"Ask it."

"What is your name?"

The Doorkeeper smiled, and said his name: and Ged, repeating it, entered for the last time into that House.

When he left it again he wore a heavy dark-blue cloak, the gift of the township of Low Torning, whereto he was bound, for they wanted a wizard there. He carried also a staff of his own height, carved of yew-wood, bronze-shod. The Doorkeeper bade him farewell opening the back door of the Great House for him, the door of horn and ivory, and he went down the streets of Thwil to a ship that waited for him on the bright water in the morning.

# CHAPTER 5

# THE DRAGON OF PENDOR

**WEST OF ROKE IN A** crowd between the two great lands Hosk and Ensmer lie the Ninety Isles. The nearest to Roke is Serd, and the farthest is Seppish, which lies almost in the Pelnish Sea; and whether the sum of them is ninety is a question never settled, for if you count only isles with freshwater springs you might have seventy, while if you count every rock you might have a hundred and still not be done; and then the tide would change. Narrow run the channels between the islets, and there the mild tides of the Inmost Sea, chafed and baffled, run high and fall low, so that where at high tide there might be three islands in one place, at low there might be one. Yet for all that danger of the tide, every child who can walk can paddle, and has his little rowboat; housewives row across the channel to take a cup of rushwash tea with the neighbor; peddlers call their wares in rhythm with the stroke of their oars. All roads there are salt water, blocked only by nets strung from house to house across the straits to catch the small fish called turbies, the oil of which is the wealth of the Ninety Isles. There are few bridges, and no great towns. Every islet is thick with farms and fishermen's houses, and these are gathered into townships each of ten or twenty islets. One such was Low Torning, the western-most, looking not on the Inmost Sea but outward to empty ocean, that lonely corner of the Archipelago where only Pendor lies, the dragon-spoiled isle, and beyond it the waters of the West Reach, desolate.

A house was ready there for the township's new wizard. It stood on a hill among green fields of barley, sheltered from the west wind by a grove of pendick-trees that now were red with flowers. From the door one looked out on other thatched roofs and groves and gardens, and other islands with their roofs and fields and hills, and amongst them all the many bright winding channels of the sea. It was a poor house, windowless, with earthen floor, yet a better house than the one Ged was born in. The Isle-Men of Low Torning, standing in awe of the wizard from Roke, asked pardon for its humbleness. "We have no stone to build with," said one, "We are none of us rich, though none starve," said another, and a third, "It will be dry at least, for I saw to the thatching myself, Sir." To Ged it was as good as any palace. He thanked the leaders of the township frankly, so that the eighteen of them went home, each in his own rowboat to his home isle, to tell the fishermen and housewives that the new wizard was a strange young grim fellow who spoke little, but he spoke fairly, and without pride.

There was little cause, perhaps, for pride in this first magistry of Ged's. Wizards trained on Roke went commonly to cities or castles, to serve high lords who held them in high honor. These fishermen of Low Torning in the usual way of things would have had among them no more than a witch or a plain sorcerer, to charm the fishing-nets and sing over new boats and cure beasts and men of their ailments. But in late years the old Dragon of Pendor had spawned: nine dragons, it was said, now laired in the ruined towers of the Sealords of Pendor, dragging their scaled bellies up and down the marble stairs and through the broken doorways there. Wanting food on that dead isle, they would be flying forth some year when they were grown and hunger came upon them. Already a flight of four had been seen over the southwest shores of Hosk, not alighting but spying out the sheepfolds, barns, and villages. The hunger of a dragon is slow to wake, but hard to sate. So the Isle-Men of Low Torning had sent to Roke begging for a wizard to protect their folk from what boded over the western horizon, and the Archmage had judged their fear well founded.

"There is no comfort in this place," the Archmage had said to Ged on the day he made him wizard, "no fame, no wealth, maybe no risk. Will you go?"

"I will go," Ged had replied; not from obedience only. Since the night on Roke Knoll his desire had turned as much against fame and display as once it had been set on them. Always now he doubted his strength and dreaded the trial of his power. Yet also the talk of dragons drew him with a great curiosity. In Gont there have been no dragons for many hundred years; and no dragon would ever fly within scent or sight or spell of Roke, so that there also they are a matter of tales and songs only, things sung of but not seen. Ged had learned all he could of dragons at the School, but it is one thing to read about dragons and another to meet them. The chance lay bright before him, and heartily he answered, "I will go."

The Archmage Gensher had nodded his head, but his look was somber. "Tell me," he said at last, "do you fear to leave Roke? or are you eager to be gone?"

"Both, my lord."

Again Gensher nodded. "I do not know if I do

right to send you from your safety here," he said very low. "I cannot see your way. It is all in darkness. And there is a power in the North, something that would destroy you, but what it is and where, whether in your past or on your forward way, I cannot tell: it is all shadowed. When the men from Low Torning came here, I thought at once of you, for it seemed a safe place and out of the way, where you might have time to gather your strength. But I do not know if any place is safe for you, or where your way goes. I do not want to send you out into the dark . . ."

It seemed a bright enough place to Ged at first, the house under the flowering trees. There he lived, and watched the western sky often, and kept his wizard's ear tuned for the sound of scaly wings. But no dragon came. Ged fished from his jetty, and tended his garden-patch. He spent whole days pondering a page or a line or a word in the Lore-Books he had brought from Roke, sitting out in the summer air under the pendick-trees, while the otak slept beside him or went hunting mice in the forests of grass and daisies. And he served the people of Low Torning as healall and weatherworker whenever they asked him. It did not enter his head that a wizard might be ashamed to perform such simple crafts, for he had been a witch-child among poorer folk than these. They, however, asked little of him, holding him in awe, partly because he was a wizard from the Isle of the Wise, and partly on account of his silence and his scarred face. There was that about him, young as he was, that made men uneasy with him.

Yet he found a friend, a boatmaker who dwelt on the next islet eastward. His name was Pechvarry. They had met first on his jetty, where Ged stopped to watch him stepping the mast of a little catboat. He had looked up at the wizard with a grin and said, "Here's a month's work nearly finished. I guess you might have done it in a minute with a word, eh, Sir?"

"I might," said Ged, "but it would likely sink the next minute, unless I kept the spells up. But if you like . . ." He stopped.

"Well, Sir?"

"Well, that is a lovely little craft. She needs nothing. But if you like, I could set a binding-spell on her, to help keep her sound; or a finding-spell, to help bring her home from the sea."

He spoke hesitantly, not wanting to offend the craftsman, but Pechvarry's face shone. "The little boat's for my son, Sir, and if you would lay such charms on her, it would be a mighty kindness and a friendly act." And he climbed up onto the jetty to take Ged's hand then and there and thank him.

After that they came to work together often,

Ged interweaving his spellcrafts with Pechvarry's handwork on the boats he built or repaired, and in return learning from Pechvarry how a boat was built, and also how a boat was handled without aid of magic: for this skill of plain sailing had been somewhat scanted on Roke. Often Ged and Pechvarry and his little son Ioeth went out into the channels and lagoons, sailing or rowing one boat or another, till Ged was a fair sailor, and the friendship between him and Pechvarry was a settled thing.

Along in late autumn the boatmaker's son fell sick. The mother sent for the witchwoman of Tesk Isle, who was a good hand at healing, and all seemed well for a day or two. Then in the middle of a stormy night came Pechvarry hammering at Ged's door, begging him to come save the child. Ged ran down to the boat with him and they rowed in all haste through dark and rain to the boatmaker's house. There Ged saw the child on his pallet-bed, and the mother crouching silent beside him, and the witchwoman making a smoke of corly-root and singing the Nagian Chant, which was the best healing she had. But she whispered to Ged, "Lord Wizard, I think this fever is the red-fever, and the child will die of it tonight."

When Ged knelt and put his hands on the child, he thought the same, and he drew back a moment.

In the latter months of his own long sickness the Master Herbal had taught him much of the healer's lore, and the first lesson and the last of all that lore was this: Heal the wound and cure the illness, but let the dying spirit go.

The mother saw his movement and the meaning of it, and cried out aloud in despair. Pechvarry stooped down by her saying, "The Lord Sparrowhawk will save him, wife. No need to cry! He's here now. He can do it."

Hearing the mother's wail, and seeing the trust Pechvarry had in him, Ged did not know how he could disappoint them. He mistrusted his own judgment, and thought perhaps the child might be saved, if the fever could be brought down. He said, "I'll do my best, Pechvarry."

He set to bathing the little boy with cold rainwater that they brought new-fallen from out of doors, and he began to say one of the spells of feverstay. The spell took no hold and made no whole, and suddenly he thought the child was dying in his arms.

Summoning his power all at once and with no thought for himself, he sent his spirit out after the child's spirit, to bring it back home. He called the child's name, "Ioeth!" Thinking some faint answer came in his inward hearing he pursued, calling once more. Then he saw the little boy running fast

and far ahead of him down a dark slope, the side
of some vast hill. There was no sound. The stars
above the hill were no stars his eyes had ever seen.
Yet he knew the constellations by name: the Sheaf,
the Door, the One Who Turns, the Tree. They
were those stars that do not set, that are not paled
by the coming of any day. He had followed the dying child too far.

Knowing this he found himself alone on the
dark hillside. It was hard to turn back, very hard.

He turned slowly. Slowly he set one foot forward to climb back up the hill, and then the other.
Step by step he went, each step willed. And each
step was harder than the last.

The stars did not move. No wind blew over
the dry steep ground. In all the vast kingdom of
the darkness only he moved, slowly, climbing. He
came to the top of the hill, and saw the low wall of
stones there. But across the wall, facing him, there
was a shadow.

The shadow did not have the shape of man or
beast. It was shapeless, scarcely to be seen, but it
whispered at him, though there were no words in
its whispering, and it reached out towards him.
And it stood on the side of the living, and he on
the side of the dead.

Either he must go down the hill into the desert
lands and lightless cities of the dead, or he must

step across the wall back into life, where the form-less evil thing waited for him.

His spirit-staff was in his hand, and he raised it high. With that motion, strength came into him. As he made to leap the low wall of stones straight at the shadow, the staff burned suddenly white, a blinding light in that dim place. He leaped, felt himself fall, and saw no more.

Now what Pechvarry and his wife and the witch saw was this: the young wizard had stopped mid-way in his spell, and held the child a while motion-less. Then he had laid little Ioeth gently down on the pallet, and had risen, and stood silent, staff in hand. All at once he raised the staff high and it blazed with white fire as if he held the lightning-bolt in his grip, and all the household things in the hut leaped out strange and vivid in that mo-mentary fire. When their eyes were clear from the dazzlement they saw the young man lying huddled forward on the earthen floor, beside the pallet where the child lay dead.

To Pechvarry it seemed that the wizard also was dead. His wife wept, but he was utterly bewildered. But the witch had some hearsay knowledge con-cerning magery and the ways a true wizard may go, and she saw to it that Ged, cold and lifeless as he lay, was not treated as a dead man but as one sick or tranced. He was carried home, and an old woman was left to watch and see whether he slept to wake or slept forever.

The little otak was hiding in the rafters of the house, as it did when strangers entered. There it stayed while the rain beat on the walls and the fire sank down and the night wearing slowly along left the old woman nodding beside the hearthpit. Then the otak crept down and came to Ged where he lay stretched stiff and still upon the bed. It began to lick his hands and wrists, long and patiently, with its dry leaf-brown tongue. Crouching beside his head it licked his temple, his scarred cheek, and softly his closed eyes. And very slowly under that soft touch Ged roused. He woke, not knowing where he had been or where he was or what was the faint grey light in the air about him, which was the light of dawn coming to the world. Then the otak curled up near his shoulder as usual, and went to sleep.

Later, when Ged thought back upon that night, he knew that had none touched him when he lay thus spirit-lost, had none called him back in some way, he might have been lost for good. It was only the dumb instinctive wisdom of the beast who licks his hurt companion to comfort him, and yet in that wisdom Ged saw something akin to his own power, something that went as deep as wizardry. From that time forth he believed that the wise man is one who never sets himself apart from other living things, whether they have speech or not, and in later years he strove long to learn what can be learned, in silence, from the eyes of animals, the flight of birds, the great slow gestures of trees.

He had now made unscathed, for the first time, that crossing-over and return which only a wizard can make with open eyes, and which not the greatest mage can make without risk. But he had returned to a grief and a fear. The grief was for his friend Pechvarry, the fear was for himself. He knew now why the Archmage had feared to send him forth, and what had darkened and clouded even the mage's foreseeing of his future. For it was darkness itself that had awaited him, the unnamed thing, the being that did not belong in the world, the shadow he had loosed or made. In spirit, at the boundary wall between death and life, it had waited for him these long years. It had found him there at last. It would be on his track now, seeking to draw near to him, to take his strength into itself, and suck up his life, and clothe itself in his flesh.

Soon after, he dreamed of the thing like a bear with no head or face. He thought it went fumbling about the walls of the house, searching for the door. Such a dream he had not dreamed since the healing of the wounds the thing had given him. When he woke he was weak and cold, and the scars on his face and shoulder drew and ached.

Now began a bad time. When he dreamed of the shadow or so much as thought of it, he felt always that same cold dread: sense and power drained out of him, leaving him stupid and astray. He raged at his cowardice, but that did no good. He sought for some protection, but there was none: the thing was not flesh, not alive, not spirit, unnamed, having no being but what he himself had given it—a terrible power outside the laws of the sunlit world. All he knew of it was that it was drawn to him and would try to work its will through him, being his creature. But in what form it could come, having no real form of its own as yet, and how it would come, and when it would come, this he did not know.

He set up what barriers of sorcery he could about his house and about the isle where he lived. Such spell-walls must be ever renewed, and soon he saw that if he spent all his strength on these defenses, he would be of no use to the islanders. What could he do, between two enemies, if a dragon came from Pendor?

Again he dreamed, but this time in the dream the shadow was inside his house, beside the door, reaching out to him through the darkness and whispering words he did not understand. He woke in terror, and sent the werelight flaming through the air, lighting every corner of the little house till he saw no shadow anywhere. Then he put wood on the coals of his firepit, and sat in the firelight hearing the autumn wind fingering at the thatch roof and whining in the great bare trees above; and he pondered long. An old anger had awakened in his heart. He would not suffer this helpless waiting, this sitting trapped on a little island muttering useless spells of lock and ward. Yet he could not simply flee the trap: to do so would be to break his trust with the islanders and to leave them to the imminent dragon, undefended. There was but one way to take.

The next morning he went down among the fishermen in the principal moorage of Low Torning, and finding the Head Isle-Man there said to him, "I must leave this place. I am in danger, and I put you in danger. I must go. Therefore I ask your leave to go out and do away with the dragons on Pendor, so that my task for you will be finished and I may leave freely. Or if I fail, I should fail also when they come here, and that is better known now than later."

The Isle-Man stared at him all dropjawed. "Lord Sparrowhawk," he said, "there are nine dragons out there!"

"Eight are still young, they say."

"But the old one—"

"I tell you, I must go from here. I ask your leave
to rid you of the dragon-peril first, if I can do so."

"As you will, Sir," the Isle-Man said gloomily.
All that listened there thought this a folly or a crazy
courage in their young wizard, and with sullen
faces they saw him go, expecting no news of him
again. Some hinted that he meant merely to sail
back by Hosk to the Inmost Sea, leaving them in
the lurch; others, among them Pechvarry, held that
he had gone mad, and sought death.

For four generations of men all ships had set
their course to keep far from the shores of Pendor
Island. No mage had ever come to do combat with
the dragon there, for the island was on no traveled
sea road, and its lords had been pirates, slavetakers,
war-makers, hated by all that dwelt in the southwest parts of Earthsea. For this reason none had
sought to revenge the Lord of Pendor, after the
dragon came suddenly out of the west upon him
and his men where they sat feasting in the tower,
and smothered them with the flames of his mouth,
and drove all the townsfolk screaming into the sea.
Unavenged, Pendor had been left to the dragon,
with all its bones, and towers, and jewels stolen
from long-dead princes of the coasts of Paln and
Hosk.

All this Ged knew well, and more, for ever since

he came to Low Torning he had held in mind and
pondered over all he had ever learned of dragons.
As he guided his small boat westward—not rowing now nor using the seaman's skill Pechvarry had
taught him, but sailing wizardly with the magewind
in his sail and a spell set on prow and keel to keep
them true—he watched to see the dead isle rise on
the rim of the sea. Speed he wanted, and therefore
used the magewind, for he feared what was behind
him more than what was before him. But as the
day passed, his impatience turned from fear to a
kind of glad fierceness. At least he sought this danger of his own will; and the nearer he came to it
the more sure he was that, for this time at least, for
this hour perhaps before his death, he was free. The
shadow dared not follow him into a dragon's jaws.
The waves ran white-tipped on the grey sea, and
grey clouds streamed overhead on the north wind.
He went west with the quick magewind in his sail,
and came in sight of the rocks of Pendor, the still
streets of the town, and the gutted, falling towers.

At the entrance of the harbor, a shallow crescent bay, he let the windspell drop and stilled his
little boat so it lay rocking on the waves. Then he
summoned the dragon: "Usurper of Pendor, come
defend your hoard!"

His voice fell short in the sound of breakers
beating on the ashen shores; but dragons have keen

ears. Presently one flitted up from some roofless ruin of the town like a vast black bat, thin-winged and spiny-backed, and circling into the north wind came flying towards Ged. His heart swelled at the sight of the creature that was a myth to his people, and he laughed and shouted, "Go tell the Old One to come, you wind-worm!"

For this was one of the young dragons, spawned there years ago by a she-dragon from the West Reach, who had set her clutch of great leathern eggs, as they say she-dragons will, in some sunny broken room of the tower and had flown away again, leaving the Old Dragon of Pendor to watch the young when they crawled like baneful lizards from the shell.

The young dragon made no answer. He was not large of his kind, maybe the length of a forty-oared ship, and was wormthin for all the reach of his black membranous wings. He had not got his growth yet, nor his voice, nor any dragon-cunning. Straight at Ged in the small rocking boat he came, opening his long, toothed jaws as he slid down arrowy from the air: so that all Ged had to do was bind his wings and limbs stiff with one sharp spell and send him thus hurtling aside into the sea like a stone falling. And the grey sea closed over him.

Two dragons like the first rose up from the base of the highest tower. Even as the first one they came driving straight at Ged, and even so he caught both, hurled both down, and drowned them; and he had not yet lifted up his wizard's staff.

Now after a little time there came three against him from the island. One of these was much greater, and fire spewed curling from its jaws. Two came flying at him rattling their wings, but the big one came circling from behind, very swift, to burn him and his boat with its breath of fire. No binding spell would catch all three, because two came from north and one from south. In the instant that he saw this, Ged worked a spell of Changing, and between one breath and the next flew up from his boat in dragon-form.

Spreading broad wings and reaching talons out, he met the two head on, withering them with fire, and then turned to the third, who was larger than he and armed also with fire. On the wind over the grey waves they doubled, snapped, swooped, lunged, till smoke roiled about them red-lit by the glare of their fiery mouths. Ged flew suddenly upward and the other pursued, below him. In mid-flight the dragon-Ged raised wings, stopped, and stooped as the hawk stoops, talons outstretched downward, striking and bearing the other down by neck and flank. The black wings flurried and black dragon-blood dropped in thick drops into the sea. The Pendor dragon tore free and flew low and lamely to the island, where it hid, crawling into some well or cavern in the ruined town.

At once Ged took his form and place again on the boat, for it was most perilous to keep that dragon-shape longer than need demanded. His hands were black with the scalding wormblood, and he was scorched about the head with fire, but this was no matter now. He waited only till he had his breath back and then called, "Six I have seen, five slain, nine are told of: come out, worms!"

No creature moved nor voice spoke for a long while on the island, but only the waves beat loudly on the shore. Then Ged was aware that the highest tower slowly changed its shape, bulging out on one side as if it grew an arm. He feared dragon-magic, for old dragons are very powerful and guileful in a sorcery like and unlike the sorcery of men: but a moment more and he saw this was no trick of the dragon, but of his own eyes. What he had taken for a part of the tower was the shoulder of the Dragon of Pendor as he uncurled his bulk and lifted himself slowly up.

When he was all afoot his scaled head, spike-crowned and triple-tongued, rose higher than the broken tower's height, and his taloned forefeet rested on the rubble of the town below. His scales were grey-black, catching the daylight like broken stone. Lean as a hound he was and huge as a hill. Ged

stared in awe. There was no song or tale could prepare the mind for this sight. Almost he stared into
the dragon's eyes and was caught, for one cannot
look into a dragon's eyes. He glanced away from
the oily green gaze that watched him, and held up
before him his staff, that looked now like a splinter,
like a twig.

"Eight sons I had, little wizard," said the great
dry voice of the dragon. "Five died, one dies:
enough. You will not win my hoard by killing
them."

"I do not want your hoard."

The yellow smoke hissed from the dragon's nostrils: that was his laughter.

"Would you not like to come ashore and look at
it, little wizard? It is worth looking at."

"No, dragon." The kinship of dragons is with
wind and fire, and they do not fight willingly over
the sea. That had been Ged's advantage so far and
he kept it; but the strip of seawater between him
and the great grey talons did not seem much of an
advantage, anymore.

It was hard not to look into the green, watching
eyes.

"You are a very young wizard," the dragon said,
"I did not know men came so young into their power." He spoke, as did Ged, in the Old Speech, for
that is the tongue of dragons still. Although the

use of the Old Speech binds a man to truth, this is not so with dragons. It is their own language, and they can lie in it, twisting the true words to false ends, catching the unwary hearer in a maze of mirrorwords each of which reflects the truth and none of which leads anywhere. So Ged had been warned often, and when the dragon spoke he listened with an untrustful ear, all his doubts ready. But the words seemed plain and clear: "Is it to ask my help that you have come here, little wizard?"

"No, dragon."

"Yet I could help you. You will need help soon, against that which hunts you in the dark."

Ged stood dumb.

"What is it that hunts you? Name it to me."

"If I could name it—" Ged stopped himself.

Yellow smoke curled above the dragon's long head, from the nostrils that were two round pits of fire.

"If you could name it you could master it, maybe, little wizard. Maybe I could tell you its name, when I see it close by. And it will come close, if you wait about my isle. It will come wherever you come. If you do not want it to come close you must run, and run, and keep running from it. And yet it will follow you. Would you like to know its name?"

Ged stood silent again. How the dragon knew

of the shadow he had loosed, he could not guess,
nor how it might know the shadow's name. The
Archmage had said that the shadow had no name.
Yet dragons have their own wisdom; and they are
an older race than man. Few men can guess what
a dragon knows and how he knows it, and those
few are the Dragonlords. To Ged, only one thing
was sure: that, though the dragon might well be
speaking truth, though he might indeed be able to
tell Ged the nature and name of the shadow-thing
and so give him power over it—even so, even if he
spoke truth, he did so wholly for his own ends.

"It is very seldom," the young man said at last,
"that dragons ask to do men favors."

"But it is very common," said the dragon, "for
cats to play with mice before they kill them."

"But I did not come here to play, or to be played
with. I came to strike a bargain with you."

Like a sword in sharpness but five times the
length of any sword, the point of the dragon's
tail arched up scorpion-wise over his mailed back,
above the tower. Dryly he spoke: "I strike no bar-
gains. I take. What have you to offer that I cannot
take from you when I like?"

"Safety. Your safety. Swear that you will never
fly eastward of Pendor, and I will swear to leave you
unharmed."

A grating sound came from the dragon's throat like the noise of an avalanche far off, stones falling among mountains. Fire danced along his three-forked tongue. He raised himself up higher, looming over the ruins. "You offer me safety! You threaten me! With what?"

"With your name, Yevaud."

Ged's voice shook as he spoke the name, yet he spoke it clear and loud. At the sound of it, the old dragon held still, utterly still. A minute went by, and another; and then Ged, standing there in his rocking chip of a boat, smiled. He had staked this venture and his life on a guess drawn from old histories of dragon-lore learned on Roke, a guess that this Dragon of Pendor was the same that had spoiled the west of Osskil in the days of Elfarran and Morred, and had been driven from Osskil by a wizard, Elt, wise in names. The guess had held.

"We are matched, Yevaud. You have the strength: I have your name. Will you bargain?"

Still the dragon made no reply.

Many years had the dragon sprawled on the island where golden breastplates and emeralds lay scattered among dust and bricks and bones; he had watched his black lizard-brood play among crumbling houses and try their wings from the cliffs; he had slept long in the sun, unwaked by voice or sail. He had grown old. It was hard now to stir, to face this mage-lad, this frail enemy, at the sight of whose staff Yevaud, the old dragon, winced.

"You may choose nine stones from my hoard," he said at last, his voice hissing and whining in his long jaws. "The best: take your choice. Then go!"

"I do not want your stones, Yevaud."

"Where is men's greed gone? Men loved bright stones in the old days in the North . . . I know what it is you want, wizard. I, too, can offer you safety, for I know what can save you. I know what alone can save you. There is a horror follows you. I will tell you its name."

Ged's heart leaped in him, and he clutched his staff, standing as still as the dragon stood. He fought a moment with sudden, startling hope.

It was not his own life that he bargained for. One mastery, and only one, could he hold over the dragon. He set hope aside and did what he must do.

"That is not what I ask for, Yevaud."

When he spoke the dragon's name it was as if he held the huge being on a fine, thin leash, tightening it on his throat. He could feel the ancient malice and experience of men in the dragon's gaze that rested on him, he could see the steel talons each as long as a man's forearm, and the stone-hard hide, and the withering fire that lurked in the dragon's throat: and yet always the leash tightened, tightened.

He spoke again: "Yevaud! Swear by your name that you and your sons will never come to the Archipelago."

Flames broke suddenly bright and loud from the dragon's jaws, and he said, "I swear it by my name!"

Silence lay over the isle then, and Yevaud lowered his great head.

When he raised it again and looked, the wizard was gone, and the sail of the boat was a white fleck on the waves eastward, heading towards the fat bejeweled islands of the inner seas. Then in rage the old Dragon of Pendor rose up breaking the tower with the writhing of his body, and beating his wings that spanned the whole width of the ruined town. But his oath held him, and he did not fly, then or ever, to the Archipelago.

# CHAPTER 6

# HUNTED

As soon as Pendor had sunk under the sea-rim behind him, Ged looking eastward felt the fear of the shadow come into his heart again; and it was hard to turn from the bright danger of the dragons to that formless, hopeless horror. He let the magewind drop, and sailed on with the world's wind, for there was no desire for speed in him now. He had no clear plan even of what he should do. He must run, as the dragon had said; but where? To Roke, he thought, since there at least he was protected, and might find counsel among the wise.

First, however, he must come to Low Torning once more and tell his tale to the Isle-Men. When word went out that he had returned, five days from his setting forth, they and half the people of the township came rowing and running to gather round him, and stare at him, and listen. He told his tale, and one man said, "But who saw this wonder of dragons slain and dragons baffled? What if he—"

"Be still!" the Head Isle-Man said roughly, for he knew, as did most of them, that a wizard may have subtle ways of telling the truth, and may keep the truth to himself, but that if he says a thing the thing is as he says. For that is his mastery. So they wondered, and began to feel that their fear was lifted from them, and then they began to rejoice. They pressed round their young wizard and asked for the tale again. More islanders came, and asked for it again. By nightfall he no longer had to tell it. They could do it for him, better. Already the village chanters had fitted it to an old tune, and were singing the *Song of the Sparrowhawk*. Bonfires were burning not only on the isles of Low Torning but in townships to the south and east. Fishermen shouted the news from boat to boat, from isle to isle it went: Evil is averted, the dragons will never come from Pendor!

That night, that one night, was joyous for Ged. No shadow could come near him through the brightness of those fires of thanksgiving that burned on every hill and beach, through the circles of laughing dancers that ringed him about, singing his praise, swinging their torches in the gusty autumn night so that sparks rose thick and bright and brief upon the wind.

The next day he met with Pechvarry, who said, "I did not know you were so mighty, my lord."

There was fear in that because he had dared make
Ged his friend, but there was reproach in it also.
Ged had not saved a little child, though he had
slain dragons. After that, Ged felt afresh the unease and impatience that had driven him to Pendor,
and drove him now from Low Torning. The next
day, though they would have kept him gladly the
rest of his life to praise and boast of, he left the
house on the hill, with no baggage but his books,
his staff, and the otak riding on his shoulder.

He went in a rowboat with a couple of young
fishermen of Low Torning, who wanted the honor
of being his boatmen. Always as they rowed on
among the craft that crowd the eastern channels
of the Ninety Isles, under the windows and bal-
conies of houses that lean out over the water, past
the wharves of Nesh, the rainy pastures of Drom-
gan, the malodorous oil-sheds of Geath, word of
his deed had gone ahead of him. They whistled the
*Song of the Sparrowhawk* as he went by, they vied to
have him spend the night and tell his dragon-tale.
When at last he came to Serd, the ship's master of
whom he asked passage out to Roke bowed as he
answered, "A privilege to me, Lord Wizard, and an
honor to my ship!"

So Ged turned his back on the Ninety Isles;
but even as the ship turned from Serd Inner Port
and raised sail, a wind came up hard from the east

against her. It was strange, for the wintry sky was clear and the weather had seemed settled mild that morning. It was only thirty miles from Serd to Roke, and they sailed on; and when the wind still rose, they still sailed on. The little ship, like most traders of the Inmost Sea, bore the high fore-and-aft sail that can be turned to catch a headwind, and her master was a handy seaman, proud of his skill. So tacking now north now south they worked eastward. Clouds and rain came up on the wind, which veered and gusted so wildly that there was considerable danger of the ship jibing. "Lord Sparrowhawk," said the ship's master to the young man, whom he had beside him in the place of honor in the stern, though small dignity could be kept up under that wind and rain that wet them all to a miserable sleekness in their sodden cloaks — "Lord Sparrowhawk, might you say a word to this wind, maybe?"

"How near are we to Roke?"

"Better than halfway. But we've made no headway at all this past hour, Sir."

Ged spoke to the wind. It blew less hard, and for a while they went on fairly enough. Then sudden great gusts came whistling out of the south, and meeting these they were driven back west-ward again. The clouds broke and boiled in the sky, and the ship's master roared out ragefully, "This fool's gale blows all ways at once! Only a magewind will get us through this weather, Lord."

Ged looked glum at that, but the ship and her men were in danger for him, so he raised up the magewind into her sail. At once the ship began to cleave straight to the east, and the ship's master began to look cheerful again. But little by little, though Ged kept up the spell, the magewind slackened, growing feebler, until the ship seemed to hang still on the waves for a minute, her sail drooping, amid all the tumult of the rain and gale. Then with a thundercrack the boom came swinging round and she jibed and jumped northward like a scared cat.

Ged grabbed hold of a stanchion, for she lay almost over on her side, and shouted out, "Turn back to Serd, master!"

The master cursed and shouted that he would not: "A wizard aboard, and I the best seaman of the Trade, and this the handiest ship I ever sailed—turn back?"

Then, the ship turning again almost as if a whirlpool had caught her keel, he too grabbed hold of the sternpost to keep aboard, and Ged said to him, "Leave me at Serd and sail where you like. It's not against your ship this wind blows, but against me."

"Against you, a wizard of Roke?"

"Have you never heard of the Roke-wind, master?"

"Aye, that keeps off evil powers from the Isle of the Wise, but what has that to do with you, a Dragontamer?"

"That is between me and my shadow," Ged answered shortly, as a wizard will; and he said no more as they went swiftly, with a steady wind and under clearing skies, back over the sea to Serd.

There was a heaviness and a dread in his heart as he went up from the wharves of Serd. The days were shortening into winter, and dusk came soon. With dusk Ged's uneasiness always grew, and now the turning of each street seemed a threat to him, and he had to steel himself not to keep looking back over his shoulder at what might be coming behind him. He went to the Sea-House of Serd, where travelers and merchants ate together of good fare provided by the township, and might sleep in the long raftered hall: such is the hospitality of the thriving islands of the Inmost Sea.

He saved a bit of meat from his dinner, and by the firepit afterward he coaxed the otak out of the fold of his hood where it had cowered all that day, and tried to get it to eat, petting it and whispering to it, "Hoeg, hoeg, little one, silent one . . ." But it would not eat, and crept into his pocket to hide. By that, by his own dull uncertainty, by the very look of the darkness in the corners of the great room, he knew that the shadow was not far from him.

No one in this place knew him: they were travelers, from other isles, who had not heard the *Song of the Sparrowhawk*. None spoke to him. He chose a pallet at last and lay down, but all night long he lay with open eyes there in the raftered hall among the sleep of strangers. All night he tried to choose his way, to plan where he should go, what he should do: but each choice, each plan was blocked by a foreboding of doom. Across each way he might go lay the shadow. Only Roke was clear of it: and to Roke he could not go, forbidden by the high, enwoven, ancient spells that kept the perilous island safe. That the Roke-wind had risen against him was proof the thing that hunted him must be very close upon him now.

That thing was bodiless, blind to sunlight, a creature of a lightless, placeless, timeless realm. It must grope after him through the days and across the seas of the sunlit world, and could take visible shape only in dream and darkness. It had as yet no substance or being that the light of the sun would shine on; and so it is sung in the *Deed of Hode*, "Daybreak makes all earth and sea, from shadow brings forth form, driving dream to the dark kingdom." But if once the shadow caught up with Ged it could draw his power out of him, and take from him the very weight and warmth and life of his body and the will that moved him.

That was the doom he saw lying ahead on every road. And he knew that he might be tricked toward that doom; for the shadow, growing stronger always as it was nearer him, might even now have strength enough to put evil powers or evil men to its own use—showing him false portents, or speaking with a stranger's voice. For all he knew, in one of these men who slept in this corner or that of the raftered hall of the Sea-House tonight, the dark thing lurked, finding a foothold in a dark soul and there waiting and watching Ged and feeding, even now, on his weakness, on his uncertainty, on his fear.

It was past bearing. He must trust to chance, and run wherever chance took him. At the first cold hint of dawn he got up and went in haste under the dimming stars down to the wharves of Serd, resolved only to take the first ship outward bound that would have him. A galley was loading turbie-oil; she was to sail at sunrise, bound for Havnor Great Port. Ged asked passage of her master. A wizard's staff is passport and payment on most ships. They took him aboard willingly, and within that hour the ship set forth. Ged's spirits lifted with the first lifting of the forty long oars, and the drumbeat that kept the stroke made a brave music to him.

And yet he did not know what he would do in Havnor, or where he would run from there. Northward was as good as any direction. He was a Northerner himself; maybe he would find some ship to take him on to Gont from Havnor, and he might see Ogion again. Or he might find some ship going far out into the Reaches, so far the shadow would lose him and give up the hunt. Beyond such vague ideas as these, there was no plan in his head, and he saw no one course that he must follow. Only he must run . . .

Those forty oars carried the ship over a hundred and fifty miles of wintry sea before sunset of the second day out from Serd. They came in to port at Orrimy on the east shore of the great land Hosk, for these trade-galleys of the Inmost Sea keep to the coasts and lie overnight in harbor whenever they can. Ged went ashore, for it was still daylight, and he roamed the steep streets of the port-town, aimless and brooding.

Orrimy is an old town, built heavily of stone and brick, walled against the lawless lords of the interior of Hosk Island; the warehouses on the docks are like forts, and the merchants' houses are towered and fortified. Yet to Ged wandering through the streets those ponderous mansions seemed like veils, behind which lay an empty dark; and people who passed him, intent on their business, seemed not real men but voiceless shadows of men. As the sun set he came down to the wharves again, and even there in the broad red light and wind of the day's end, sea and land alike to him seemed dim and silent.

"Where are you bound, Lord Wizard?"

So one hailed him suddenly from behind. Turning he saw a man dressed in grey, who carried a staff of heavy wood that was not a wizard's staff. The stranger's face was hidden by his hood from the red light, but Ged felt the unseen eyes meet his. Starting back he raised his own yew-staff between him and the stranger.

Mildly the man asked, "What do you fear?"

"What follows behind me."

"So? But I'm not your shadow."

Ged stood silent. He knew that indeed this man, whatever he was, was not what he feared: he was no shadow or ghost or gebbeth-creature. Amidst the dry silence and shadowiness that had come over the world, he even kept a voice and some solidity. He put back his hood now. He had a strange, seamed, bald head, a lined face. Though age had not sounded in his voice, he looked to be an old man.

"I do not know you," said the man in grey, "yet I think perhaps we do not meet by chance. I heard a tale once of a young man, a scarred man, who won through darkness to great dominion, even to kingship. I do not know if that is your tale. But I will tell you this: go to the Court of the Terrenon, if you need a sword to fight shadows with. A staff of yew-wood will not serve your need."

Hope and mistrust struggled in Ged's mind as he listened. A wizardly man soon learns that few indeed of his meetings are chance ones, be they for good or for ill.

"In what land is the Court of the Terrenon?"

"In Osskil."

At the sound of that name Ged saw for a moment, by a trick of memory, a black raven on green grass who looked up at him sidelong with an eye like polished stone, and spoke; but the words were forgotten.

"That land has something of a dark name," Ged said, looking ever at the man in grey, trying to judge what kind of man he was. There was a manner about him that hinted of the sorcerer, even of the wizard; and yet boldly as he spoke to Ged, there was a queer beaten look about him, the look almost of a sick man, or a prisoner, or a slave.

"You are from Roke," he answered. "The wizards of Roke give a dark name to wizardries other than their own."

"What man are you?"

"A traveler; a trader's agent from Osskil; I am

here on business," said the man in grey. When Ged asked him no more he quietly bade the young man good night, and went off up the narrow stepped street above the quays.

Ged turned, irresolute whether to heed this sign or not, and looked to the north. The red light was dying out fast from the hills and from the windy sea. Grey dusk came, and on its heels the night.

Ged went in sudden decision and haste along the quays to a fisherman who was folding his nets down in his dory, and hailed him: "Do you know any ship in this port bound north—to Semel, or the Enlades?"

"The longship yonder's from Osskil, she might be stopping at the Enlades."

In the same haste Ged went on to the great ship the fisherman had pointed to, a longship of sixty oars, gaunt as a snake, her high bent prow carven and inlaid with disks of loto-shell, her oarport-covers painted red, with the rune Sifl sketched on each in black. A grim, swift ship she looked, and all in sea-trim, with all her crew aboard. Ged sought out the ship's master and asked passage to Osskil of him.

"Can you pay?"

"I have some skill with winds."

"I am a weatherworker myself. You have nothing to give? No money?"

In Low Torning the Isle-Men had paid Ged as best they could with the ivory pieces used by traders in the Archipelago; he would take only ten pieces, though they wanted to give him more. He offered these now to the Osskilian, but he shook his head. "We do not use those counters. If you have nothing to pay, I have no place aboard for you."

"Do you need arms? I have rowed in a galley."

"Aye, we're short two men. Find your bench then," said the ship's master, and paid him no more heed.

So, laying his staff and his bag of books under the rowers' bench, Ged became for ten bitter days of winter an oarsman of that Northern ship. They left Orrimy at daybreak, and that day Ged thought he could never keep up his work. His left arm was somewhat lamed by the old wounds in his shoulder, and all his rowing in the channels about Low Torning had not trained him for the relentless pull and pull and pull at the long galley-oar to the beat of the drum. Each stint at the oars was of two or three hours, and then a second shift of oarsmen took the benches, but the time of rest seemed only long enough for all Ged's muscles to stiffen, and then it was back to the oars. And the second day of it was worse; but after that he hardened to the labor, and got on well enough.

There was no such comradeship among this

crew as he had found aboard *Shadow* when he first went to Roke. The crewmen of Andradean and Gontish ships are partners in the trade, working together for a common profit, whereas traders of Osskil use slaves and bondsmen or hire men to row, paying them with small coins of gold. Gold is a great thing in Osskil. But it is not a source of good fellowship there, or amongst the dragons, who also prize it highly. Since half this crew were bondsmen, forced to work, the ship's officers were slavemasters, and harsh ones. They never laid their whips on the back of an oarsman who worked for pay or passage; but there will not be much friendliness in a crew of whom some are whipped and others are not. Ged's fellows said little to one another, and less to him. They were mostly men from Osskil, speaking not the Hardic tongue of the Archipelago but a dialect of their own, and they were dour men, pale-skinned with black drooping mustaches and lank hair. *Kelub,* the red one, was Ged's name among them. Though they knew he was a wizard they showed him no regard, but rather a kind of cautious spitefulness. And he himself was in no mood for making friends. Even on his bench, caught up in the mighty rhythm of the rowing, one oarsman among sixty in a ship racing over void grey seas, he felt himself exposed, defenseless. When they came into strange ports at nightfall and he rolled himself in his cloak to sleep, weary as he was he would dream, wake, dream again: evil dreams, that he could not recall waking, though they seemed to hang about the ship and the men of the ship, so that he mistrusted each one of them.

All the Osskilian freemen wore a long knife at the hip, and one day as his oar-shift shared their noon meal one of these men asked Ged, "Are you slave or oathbreaker, Kelub?"

"Neither."

"Why no knife, then? Afraid to fight?" said the man, Skiorh, jeering.

"No."

"Your little dog fight for you?"

"Otak," said another who listened. "No dog, that is otak," and he said something in Osskilian that made Skiorh scowl and turn away. Just as he turned Ged saw a change in his face, a slurring and shifting of the features, as if for a moment something had changed him, used him, looking out through his eyes sidelong at Ged. Yet the next minute Ged saw him full-face, and he looked as usual, so that Ged told himself that what he had seen was his own fear, his own dread reflected in the other's eyes. But that night as they lay in port in Esen he dreamed, and Skiorh walked in his dream. Afterwards he avoided the man as best he could, and it seemed also that Skiorh kept away from him, and no more words passed between them.

The snow-crowned mountains of Havnor sank away behind them southward, blurred by the mists of early winter. They rowed on past the mouth of the Sea of Éa where long ago Elfarran was drowned, and past the Enlades. They lay two days in port at Berila, the City of Ivory, white above its bay in the west of myth-haunted Enlad. At all ports they came to, the crewmen were kept aboard the ship, and set no foot on land. Then as a red sun rose they rowed out on the Osskil Sea, into the north-east winds that blow unhindered from the island-less vastness of the North Reach. Through that bitter sea they brought their cargo safe, coming the second day out of Berila into port at Neshum, the trade-city of Eastern Osskil.

Ged saw a low coast lashed by rainy wind, a grey town crouching behind the long stone breakwaters that made its harbor, and behind the town treeless hills under a snow-darkened sky. They had come far from the sunlight of the Inmost Sea.

Longshoremen of the Sea-Guild of Neshum came aboard to unload the cargo—gold, silver, jewelry, fine silks and Southern tapestries, such precious stuff as the lords of Osskil hoard—and the

freemen of the crew were dismissed. Ged stopped
one of them to ask his way; up until now the dis-
trust he felt of all of them had kept him from saying where he was bound, but now, afoot and alone
in a strange land, he must ask for guidance. The
man went on impatiently saying he did not know,
but Skiorh, overhearing, said, "The Court of the
Terrenon? On the Keksemt Moors. I go that road."

Skiorh's was no company Ged would have chosen, but knowing neither the language nor the way
he had small choice. Nor did it much matter, he
thought; he had not chosen to come here. He had
been driven, and now was driven on. He pulled his
hood up over his head, took up his staff and bag,
and followed the Osskilian through the streets of
the town and upward into the snowy hills. The little otak would not ride on his shoulder, but hid in
the pocket of his sheepskin tunic, under his cloak,
as was its wont in cold weather. The hills stretched
out into bleak rolling moorlands as far as the eye
could see. They walked in silence and the silence of
winter lay on all the land.

"How far?" Ged asked after they had gone some
miles, seeing no sight of village or farm in any direction, and thinking that they had no food with
them. Skiorh turned his head a moment, pulling
up his own hood, and said, "Not far."

It was an ugly face, pale, coarse, and cruel, but Ged feared no man, though he might fear where such a man would guide him. He nodded, and they went on. Their road was only a scar through the waste of thin snow and leafless bushes. From time to time other tracks crossed it or branched from it. Now that the chimney-smoke of Neshum was hidden behind the hills in the darkening afternoon there was no sign at all of what way they should go, or had gone. Only the wind blew always from the east. And when they had walked for several hours Ged thought he saw, away off on the hills in the northwest where their way tended, a tiny scratch against the sky, like a tooth, white. But the light of the short day was fading, and on the next rise of the road he could make out the thing, tower or tree or whatever, no more clearly than before.

"Do we go there?" he asked, pointing.

Skiorh made no answer but plodded on, muffled in his coarse cloak with its peaked, furred Osskilian hood. Ged strode on beside him. They had come far, and he was drowsy with the steady pace of their walking and with the long weariness of hard days and nights in the ship. It began to seem to him that he had walked forever and would walk forever beside this silent being through a silent darkening land. Caution and intention were dulled in him. He walked as in a long, long dream, going no place.

The otak stirred in his pocket, and a little vague fear also woke and stirred in his mind. He forced himself to speak. "Darkness comes, and snow. How far, Skiorh?"

After a pause the other answered, without turning, "Not far."

But his voice sounded not like a man's voice, but like a beast, hoarse and lipless, that tries to speak.

Ged stopped. All around stretched empty hills in the late, dusk light. Sparse snow whirled a little falling. "Skiorh!" he said, and the other halted, and turned. There was no face under the peaked hood.

Before Ged could speak spell or summon power, the gebbeth spoke, saying in its hoarse voice, "Ged!"

Then the young man could work no transformation, but was locked in his true being, and must face the gebbeth thus defenseless. Nor could he summon any help in this alien land, where nothing and no one was known to him and would come at his call. He stood alone, with nothing between him and his enemy but the staff of yew-wood in his right hand.

The thing that had devoured Skiorh's mind and possessed his flesh made the body take a step towards Ged, and the arms came groping out towards him. A rage of horror filled Ged and he swung up and brought down his staff whistling on the hood that hid the shadow-face. Hood and cloak collapsed down nearly to the ground under that fierce blow as if there was nothing in them but wind, and then writhing and flapping stood up again. The body of a gebbeth has been drained of true substance and is something like a shell or a vapor in the form of a man, an unreal flesh clothing the shadow which is real. So jerking and billowing as if blown on the wind the shadow spread its arms and came at Ged, trying to get hold of him as it had held him on Roke Knoll: and if it did it would cast aside the husk of Skiorh and enter into Ged, devouring him out from within, owning him, which was its whole desire. Ged struck at it again with his heavy, smoking staff, beating it off, but it came again and he struck again, and then dropped the staff that blazed and smoldered, burning his hand. He backed away, then all at once turned and ran.

He ran, and the gebbeth followed a pace behind him, unable to outrun him yet never dropping behind. Ged never looked back. He ran, he ran, through that vast dusk land where there was no hiding place. Once the gebbeth in its hoarse whistling voice called him again by name, but though it had taken his wizard's power thus, it had no power over his body's strength, and could not make him stop. He ran.

Night thickened about the hunter and the hunted, and snow blew fine across the path that Ged could no longer see. The pulse hammered in his eyes, the breath burned in his throat, he was no longer really running but stumbling and staggering ahead: and yet the tireless pursuer seemed unable to catch up, coming always just behind him. It had begun to whisper and mumble at him, calling to him, and he knew that all his life that whispering had been in his ears, just under the threshold of hearing, but now he could hear it, and he must yield, he must give in, he must stop. Yet he labored on, struggling up a long, dim slope. He thought there was a light somewhere before him, and he thought he heard a voice in front of him, above him somewhere, calling, "Come! Come!"

He tried to answer but he had no voice. The pale light grew certain, shining through a gateway straight before him: he could not see the walls, but he saw the gate. At the sight of it he halted, and the gebbeth snatched at his cloak, fumbled at his sides trying to catch hold of him from behind. With the last strength in him Ged plunged through that faint-shining door. He tried to turn to shut it behind him against the gebbeth, but his legs would not hold him up. He staggered, reaching for support. Lights swam and flashed in his eyes. He felt himself falling, and he felt himself caught even as he fell; but his mind, utterly spent, slid away into the dark.

# CHAPTER 7

# THE HAWK'S FLIGHT

GED WOKE, AND FOR A long time he lay, aware only that it was pleasant to wake, for he had not expected to wake again, and very pleasant to see light, the large plain light of day all about him. He felt as if he were floating on that light, or drifting in a boat on very quiet waters. At last he made out that he was in bed, but no such bed as he had ever slept in. It was set up on a frame held by four tall carven legs, and the mattresses were great silk sacks of down, which was why he thought he was floating, and over it all a crimson canopy hung to keep out drafts. On two sides the curtain was tied back, and Ged looked out at a room with walls of stone and floor of stone. Through three high windows he saw the moorland, bare and brown, snow-patched here and there, in the mild sunlight of winter. The room must be high above the ground, for it looked a great way over the land.

A coverlet of downfilled satin slid aside as Ged sat up, and he saw himself clothed in a tunic of silk

and cloth-of-silver like a lord. On a chair beside the
bed, boots of glove-leather and a cloak lined with
pellawi-fur were laid ready for him. He sat a while,
calm and dull as one under an enchantment, and
then stood up, reaching for his staff. But he had no
staff.

His right hand, though it had been salved and
bound, was burned on palm and fingers. Now he
felt the pain of it, and the soreness of all his body.

He stood without moving a while again. Then
he whispered, not aloud and not hopefully, "Hoeg
. . . hoeg . . ." For the little fierce loyal creature too
was gone, the little silent soul that once had led
him back from death's dominion. Had it still been
with him last night when he ran? Was that last
night, was it many nights ago? He did not know. It
was all dim and obscure in his mind, the gebbeth,
the burning staff, the running, the whispering, the
gate. None of it came back clearly to him. Nothing
even now was clear. He whispered his pet's name
once more, but without hope of answer, and tears
rose in his eyes.

A little bell rang somewhere far away. A second
bell rang in a sweet jangle just outside the room.
A door opened behind him, across the room, and
a woman came in. "Welcome, Sparrowhawk," she
said, smiling.

She was young and tall, dressed in white and silver, with a net of silver crowning her hair that fell straight down like a fall of black water.

Stiffly Ged bowed.

"You don't remember me, I think."

"Remember you, Lady?"

He had never seen a beautiful woman dressed to match her beauty but once in his life: that Lady of O who had come with her Lord to the Sunreturn festival at Roke. She had been like a slight, bright candle-flame, but this woman was like the white new moon.

"I thought you would not," she said smiling. "But forgetful as you may be, you're welcome here as an old friend."

"What place is this?" Ged asked, still stiff and slow-tongued. He found it hard to speak to her and hard to look away from her. The princely clothes he wore were strange to him, the stones he stood on were unfamiliar, the very air he breathed was alien; he was not himself, not the self he had been.

"This keep is called the Court of the Terrenon. My lord, who is called Benderesk, is sovereign of this land from the edge of the Keksemt Moors north to the Mountains of Os, and keeper of the precious stone called Terrenon. As for myself, here in Osskil they call me Serret, Silver in their lan-

guage. And you, I know, are sometimes called
Sparrowhawk, and were made wizard in the Isle of
the Wise."

Ged looked down at his burned hand and said
presently, "I do not know what I am. I had power,
once. I have lost it, I think."

"No! You have not lost it, or only to regain it
tenfold. You are safe here from what drove you here,
my friend. There are mighty walls about this tower
and not all of them are built of stone. Here you can
rest, finding your strength again. Here you may
also find a different strength, and a staff that will
not burn to ashes in your hand. An evil way may
lead to a good end, after all. Come with me now,
let me show you our domain."

She spoke so sweetly that Ged hardly heard her
words, moved by the promise of her voice alone.
He followed her.

His room was high up indeed in the tower that
rose like a sharp tooth from its hilltop. Down winding stairs of marble he followed Serret, through rich
rooms and halls, past high windows that looked
north, west, south, east over the low brown hills
that went on, houseless and treeless and changeless,
clear to the sunwashed winter sky. Only far to the
north small white peaks stood sharp against the
blue, and southward one could guess the shining of
the sea.

Servants opened doors and stood aside for Ged and the lady; pale, dour Osskilians they were all. She was light of skin, but unlike them she spoke Hardic well, even, it seemed to Ged, with the accent of Gont. Later that day she brought him before her husband Benderesk, Lord of the Terrenon. Thrice her age, bone-white, bone-thin, with clouded eyes, Lord Benderesk greeted Ged with grim cold courtesy, bidding him stay as guest however long he would. Then he had little more to say, asking Ged nothing of his voyages or of the enemy that had hunted him here; nor had the Lady Serret asked anything of these matters.

If this was strange, it was only part of the strangeness of this place and of his presence in it. Ged's mind never seemed quite to clear. He could not see things plainly. He had come to this tower-keep by chance, and yet the chance was all design; or he had come by design and yet all the design had merely chanced to come about. He had set out northward; a stranger in Orrimy had told him to seek help here; an Osskilian ship had been waiting for him; Skiorh had guided him. How much of this was the work of the shadow that hunted him? Or was none of it; had he and his hunter both been drawn here by some other power, he following that lure and the shadow following him, and seizing on Skiorh for its weapon when the moment came? That must be it, for certainly the shadow was, as Serret had said, barred from the Court of the Terrenon. He had felt no sign or threat of its lurking presence since he wakened in the tower. But what then had brought him here? For this was no place one came to by chance; even in the dullness of his thoughts he began to see that. No other stranger came to these gates. The tower stood aloof and remote, its back turned on the way to Neshum that was the nearest town. No man came to the keep, none left it. Its windows looked down on desolation.

From these windows Ged looked out, as he kept by himself in his high tower-room, day after day, dull and heartsick and cold. It was always cold in the tower, for all the carpets and the tapestried hangings and the rich furred clothing and the broad marble fireplaces they had. It was a cold that got into the bone, into the marrow, and would not be dislodged. And in Ged's heart a cold shame settled also and would not be dislodged, as he thought always how he had faced his enemy and been defeated and had run. In his mind all the Masters of Roke gathered, Gensher the Archmage frowning in their midst, and Nemmerle was with them, and Ogion, and even the witch who had taught him his first spell: all of them gazed at him and he knew he had failed their trust in him. He would plead, saying, "If I had not run away the shadow would have possessed me: it had already all Skiorh's strength, and part of mine, and I could not fight it: it knew my name. I had to run away. A wizard-gebbeth would be a terrible power for evil and ruin. I had to run away." But none of those who listened in his mind would answer him. And he would watch the snow falling, thin and ceaseless, on the empty lands below the window, and feel the dull cold grow within him, till it seemed no feeling was left to him except a kind of weariness.

So he kept to himself for many days out of sheer misery. When he did come down out of his room, he was silent and stiff. The beauty of the Lady of the Keep confused his mind, and in this rich, seemly, orderly, strange Court, he felt himself to be a goatherd born and bred.

They let him alone when he wanted to be alone, and when he could not stand to think his thoughts and watch the falling snow any longer, often Serret met with him in one of the curving halls, tapestried and firelit, lower in the tower, and there they would talk. There was no merriment in the Lady of the Keep, she never laughed though she often smiled; yet she could put Ged at ease almost with one smile. With her he began to forget his stiffness and his shame. Before long they met every day to talk, long, quietly, idly, a little apart from the serving-women who always accompanied Serret, by the fireplace or at the window of the high rooms of the tower.

The old lord kept mostly in his own apartments, coming forth mornings to pace up and down the snowy inner courtyards of the castle-keep like an old sorcerer who has been brewing spells all night. When he joined Ged and Serret for supper he sat silent, looking up at his young wife sometimes with a hard, covetous glance. Then Ged pitied her. She was like a white deer caged, like a white bird wing-clipped, like a silver ring on an old man's finger. She was an item of Benderesk's hoard. When the Lord of the Keep left them Ged stayed with her, trying to cheer her solitude as she had cheered his.

"What is this jewel that gives your keep its name?" he asked her as they sat talking over their emptied gold plates and gold goblets in the carvernous, candle-lit dining-hall.

"You have not heard of it? It is a famous thing."

"No. I know only that the lords of Osskil have famous treasuries."

"Ah, this jewel outshines them all. Come, would you like to see it?"

She smiled, with a look of mockery and daring, as if a little afraid of what she did, and led the young man from the hall, out through the narrow corridors of the base of the tower, and down stairs underground to a locked door he had not seen before. This she unlocked with a silver key, looking up at Ged with that same smile as she did so, as if she dared him to come on with her. Beyond the door was a short passage and a second door, which she unlocked with a gold key, and beyond that again a third door, which she unlocked with one of the Great Words of unbinding. Within that last door her candle showed them a small room like a dungeon-cell: floor, walls, ceiling all rough stone, unfurnished, blank.

"Do you see it?" Serret asked.

As Ged looked round the room his wizard's eye caught one stone of those that made the floor. It was rough and dank as the rest, a heavy unshapen paving-stone: yet he felt the power of it as if it spoke to him aloud. And his breath caught in his throat, and a sickness came over him for a moment. This was the foundingstone of the tower. This was the central place, and it was cold, bitter cold; nothing could ever warm the little room. This was a very ancient thing: an old and terrible spirit was prisoned in that block of stone. He did not answer Serret yes or no, but stood still, and presently, with a quick curious glance at him, she pointed out the stone. "That is the Terrenon. Do you wonder that we keep so precious a jewel locked away in our deepest hoardroom?"

Still Ged did not answer, but stood dumb and wary. She might almost have been testing him; but he thought she had no notion of the stone's nature, to speak of it so lightly. She did not know enough of it to fear it. "Tell me of its powers," he said at last.

"It was made before Segoy raised the islands of the world from the Open Sea. It was made when the world itself was made, and will endure until the end of the world. Time is nothing to it. If you lay your hand upon it and ask a question of it, it will answer, according to the power that is in you. It has a voice, if you know how to listen. It will speak of things that were, and are, and will be. It told of your coming, long before you came to this land. Will you ask a question of it now?"

"No."

"It will answer you."

"There is no question I would ask it."

"It might tell you," Serret said in her soft voice, "how you will defeat your enemy."

Ged stood mute.

"Do you fear the stone?" she asked as if unbelieving; and he answered, "Yes."

In the deadly cold and silence of the room encircled by wall after wall of spellwork and of stone, in the light of the one candle she held, Serret glanced at him again with gleaming eyes. "Sparrowhawk," she said, "you are not afraid."

"But I will not speak with that spirit," Ged replied, and looking full at her spoke with a grave boldness: "My lady, that spirit is sealed in a stone, and the stone is locked by binding-spell and blinding-spell and charm of lock and ward and triple fortress-walls in a barren land, not because it is precious, but because it can work great evil. I do not know what they told you of it when you came here. But you who are young and gentle-hearted should never touch the thing, or even look on it. It will not work you well."

"I have touched it. I have spoken to it, and heard it speak. It does me no harm."

She turned away and they went out through the doors and passages till in the torchlight of the broad stairs of the tower she blew out her candle. They parted with few words.

That night Ged slept little. It was not the thought of the shadow that kept him awake; rather that thought was almost driven from his mind by the image, ever returning, of the Stone on which this tower was founded, and by the vision of Serret's face bright and shadowy in the candle-light, turned to him. Again and again he felt her eyes on him, and tried to decide what look had come into those eyes when he refused to touch the Stone, whether it had been disdain or hurt. When he lay down to sleep at last the silken sheets of the bed were cold as ice, and ever he wakened in the dark thinking of the Stone and of Serret's eyes.

Next day he found her in the curving hall of grey marble, lit now by the westering sun, where often she spent the afternoon at games or at the weaving-loom with her maids. He said to her, "Lady Serret, I affronted you. I am sorry for it."

"No," she said musingly, and again, "No . . ." She sent away the serving-women who were with her, and when they were alone she turned to Ged. "My guest, my friend," she said, "you are very clear-sighted, but perhaps you do not see all that is to be seen. In Gont, in Roke, they teach high wizardries. But they do not teach all wizardries. This is Osskil, Ravenland: it is not a Hardic land: mages do not rule it, nor do they know much of it. There are happenings here not dealt with by the loremasters of the South, and things here not named in the Namers' lists. What one does not know, one fears. But you have nothing to fear here in the Court of the Terrenon. A weaker man would, indeed. Not you. You are one born with the power to control that which is in the sealed room. This I know. It is why you are here now."

"I do not understand."

"That is because my lord Benderesk has not been wholly frank with you. I will be frank. Come, sit by me here."

He sat down beside her on the deep, cushioned window-ledge. The dying sunlight came level through the window, flooding them with a radiance in which there was no warmth; on the moorlands below, already sinking into shadow, last night's snow lay unmelted, a dull white pall over the earth.

She spoke now very softly. "Benderesk is Lord and Inheritor of the Terrenon, but he cannot use the thing, he cannot make it wholly serve his will. Nor can I, alone or with him. Neither he nor I has the skill and power. You have both."

"How do you know that?"

"From the Stone itself! I told you that it spoke of your coming. It knows its master. It has waited for you to come. Before ever you were born it waited for you, for the one who could master it. And he who can make the Terrenon answer what he asks and do what he wills, has power over his own destiny: strength to crush any enemy, mortal or of the other world: foresight, knowledge, wealth, dominion, and a wizardry at his command that could humble the Archmage himself! As much of that, as little of that as you choose, is yours for the asking."

Once more she lifted her strange bright eyes to him, and her gaze pierced him so that he trembled as if with cold. Yet there was fear in her face, as if she sought his help but was too proud to ask it. Ged was bewildered. She had put her hand on his as she spoke; its touch was light, it looked narrow and fair on his dark, strong hand. He said, pleading, "Serret! I have no such power as you think—what I had once, I threw away. I cannot help you, I am no use to you. But I know this: the Old Powers of earth are not for men to use. They were never given into our hands, and in our hands they work only ruin. Ill means, ill end. I was not drawn here, but driven here, and the force that drove me works to my undoing. I cannot help you."

"He who throws away his power is filled sometimes with a far greater power," she said, smiling, as if his fears and scruples were childish ones. "I may know more than you of what brought you here. Did not a man speak to you in the streets of Orrimy? He was a messenger, a servant of the Terrenon. He was a wizard once himself, but he threw away his staff to serve a power greater than any mage's. And you came to Osskil, and on the moors you tried to fight a shadow with your wooden staff; and almost we could not save you, for that thing that follows you is more cunning than we deemed, and had taken much strength from you already . . . Only shadow can fight shadow. Only darkness can defeat the dark. Listen, Sparrowhawk! what do you need, then, to defeat that shadow, which waits for you outside these walls?"

"I need what I cannot know. Its name."

"The Terrenon, that knows all births and deaths and beings before and after death, the unborn and the undying, the bright world and the dark one, will tell you that name."

"And the price?"

"There is no price. I tell you it will obey you, serve you as your slave."

Shaken and tormented, he did not answer. She held his hand now in both of hers, looking into his face. The sun had fallen into the mists that dulled the horizon, and the air too had grown dull, but her face grew bright with praise and triumph as she watched him and saw his will shaken within him. Softly she whispered, "You will be mightier than all men, a king among men. You will rule, and I will rule with you—"

Suddenly Ged stood up, and one step forward took him where he could see, just around the curve of the long room's wall, beside the door, the Lord of the Terrenon who stood listening and smiling a little.

Ged's eyes cleared, and his mind. He looked down at Serret. "It is light that defeats the dark," he said stammering, — "light."

As he spoke he saw, as plainly as if his own words were the light that showed him, how indeed he had been drawn here, lured here, how they had used his fear to lead him on, and how they would, once they had him, have kept him. They had saved him from the shadow, indeed, for they did not want him to be possessed by the shadow until he had become a slave of the Stone. Once his will was captured by the power of the Stone, then they would let the shadow into the walls, for a gebbeth was a better slave even than a man. If he had once touched the Stone, or spoken to it, he would have been utterly lost. Yet, even as the shadow had not quite been able to catch up with him and seize him, so the Stone had not been able to use him — not quite. He had almost yielded, but not quite. He had not consented. It is very hard for evil to take hold of the unconsenting soul.

He stood between the two who had yielded, who had consented, looking from one to the other as Benderesk came forward.

"I told you," the Lord of the Terrenon said dry-voiced to his lady, "that he would slip from your hands, Serret. They are clever fools, your Gontish sorcerers. And you are a fool too, woman of Gont, thinking to trick both him and me, and rule us both by your beauty, and use the Terrenon to your own ends. But I am the Lord of the Stone, I, and this I do to the disloyal wife: *Ekavroe ai oelwant-ar*—" It was a spell of Changing, and Benderesk's long hands were raised to shape the cowering woman into some hideous thing, swine or dog or driveling hag. Ged stepped forward and struck the lord's hands down with his own, saying as he did so only one short word. And though he had no staff, and stood on alien ground and evil ground, the domain of a dark power, yet his will prevailed. Benderesk stood still, his clouded eyes fixed hateful and unseeing upon Serret.

"Come," she said in a shaking voice, "Sparrowhawk, come, quick, before he can summon the Servants of the Stone—"

As if in echo a whispering ran through the tower, through the stones of the floor and walls, a dry trembling murmur, as if the earth itself should speak.

Seizing Ged's hand Serret ran with him through the passages and halls, down the long twisted stairs. They came out into the courtyard where a last silvery daylight still hung above the soiled, trodden snow. Three of the castle-servants barred their way, sullen and questioning, as if they had been suspecting some plot of these two against their master. "It grows dark, Lady," one said, and another, "You cannot ride out now."

"Out of my way, filth!" Serret cried, and spoke in the sibilant Osskilian speech. The men fell back from her and crouched down to the ground, writhing, and one of them screamed aloud.

"We must go out by the gate, there is no other way out. Can you see it? can you find it, Sparrowhawk?"

She tugged at his hand, yet he hesitated. "What spell did you set on them?"

"I ran hot lead in the marrow of their bones, they will die of it. Quick, I tell you, he will loose the Servants of the Stone, and I cannot find the gate—there is a great charm on it. Quick!"

Ged did not know what she meant, for to him the enchanted gate was as plain to see as the stone archway of the court through which he saw it. He led Serret through the one, across the untrodden snow of the forecourt, and then, speaking a word of Opening, he led her through the gate of the wall of spells.

She changed as they passed through that doorway out of the silvery twilight of the Court of the Terrenon. She was not less beautiful in the drear light of the moors, but there was a fierce witch-look to her beauty; and Ged knew her at last—the daughter of the Lord of the Re Albi, daughter of a sorceress of Osskil, who had mocked him in the green meadows above Ogion's house, long ago, and had sent him to read that spell which loosed the shadow. But he spent small thought on this, for he was looking about him now with every sense alert, looking for that enemy, the shadow, which would be waiting for him somewhere outside the magic walls. It might be gebbeth still, clothed in Skiorh's death, or it might be hidden in the gathering darkness, waiting to seize him and merge its shapelessness with his living flesh. He sensed its nearness, yet did not see it. But as he looked he saw some small dark thing half buried in snow, a few paces from the gate. He stooped, and then softly picked it up in his two hands. It was the otak, its fine short fur all clogged with blood and its small body light and stiff and cold in his hands.

"Change yourself! Change yourself, they are coming!" Serret shrieked, seizing his arm and pointing to the tower that stood behind them like a tall white tooth in the dusk. From slit windows near its base dark creatures were creeping forth, flapping long wings, slowly beating and circling up over the walls towards Ged and Serret where they stood on the hillside, unprotected. The rattling whisper they had heard inside the keep had grown louder, a tremor and moaning in the earth under their feet.

Anger welled up in Ged's heart, a hot rage of hate against all the cruel deathly things that tricked him, trapped him, hunted him down. "Change yourself!" Serret screamed at him, and she with a quick-gasped spell shrank into a grey gull, and flew. But Ged stooped and plucked a blade of wild grass that poked up dry and frail out of the snow where the otak had lain dead. This blade he held up, and as he spoke aloud to it in the True Speech it lengthened, and thickened, and when he was done he held a great staff, a wizard's staff, in his hand. No banefire burned red along it when the black, flapping creatures from the Court of the Terrenon swooped over him and he struck their wings with it: it blazed only with the white magefire that does not burn but drives away the dark.

The creatures returned to the attack: botched beasts, belonging to ages before bird or dragon or man, long since forgotten by the daylight but recalled by the ancient, malign, unforgetful power of the Stone. They harried Ged, swooping at him. He felt the scythe-sweep of their talons about him and sickened in their dead stench. Fiercely he parried and struck, fighting them off with the fiery staff that was made of his anger and a blade of wild grass. And suddenly they all rose up like ravens frightened from carrion and wheeled away, flapping, silent, in the direction that Serret in her gullshape had flown. Their vast wings seemed slow, but they flew fast, each downbeat driving them mightily through the air. No gull could long outmatch that heavy speed.

Quick as he had once done at Roke, Ged took the shape of a great hawk: not the sparrowhawk they called him but the Pilgrim Falcon that flies like an arrow, like thought. On barred, sharp, strong wings he flew, pursuing his pursuers. The air darkened and among the clouds stars shone brightening. Ahead he saw the black ragged flock all driving down and in upon one point in mid-air. Beyond that black clot the sea lay, pale with the last ashy gleam of day. Swift and straight the hawk-Ged shot towards the creatures of the Stone, and they scattered as he came amongst them as waterdrops scatter from a cast pebble. But they had caught their prey. Blood was on the beak of this one and white feathers stuck to the claws of another, and no gull skimmed beyond them over the pallid sea.

Already they were turning on Ged again, coming quick and ungainly with iron beaks stretched out agape. He, wheeling once above them, screamed the hawk's scream of defiant rage, and then shot on across the low beaches of Osskil, out over the breakers of the sea.

The creatures of the Stone circled a while croaking, and one by one beat back ponderously inland over the moors. The Old Powers will not cross over the sea, being bound each to an isle, a certain place, cave or stone or welling spring. Back went the black emanations to the tower-keep, where maybe the Lord of the Terrenon, Benderesk, wept at their return, and maybe laughed. But Ged went on, falcon-winged, falcon-mad, like an unfalling arrow, like an unforgotten thought, over the Osskil Sea and eastward into the wind of winter and the night.

OGION THE SILENT HAD COME home late to Re Albi from his autumn wanderings. More silent, more solitary than ever he had become as the years went on. The new Lord of Gont down in the city below had never got a word out of him, though he had climbed clear up to the Falcon's Nest to seek the help of the mage in a certain piratic venture towards the Andrades. Ogion who spoke to spiders on their webs and had been seen to greet trees courteously never said a word to the Lord of the Isle, who went away discontented. There was perhaps some discontent or unease also in Ogion's mind, for he had spent all summer and autumn alone up on the mountain, and only now near Sunreturn was come back to his hearthside.

The morning after his return he rose late, and wanting a cup of rushwash tea he went out to fetch water from the spring that ran a little way down the hillside from his house. The margins of the spring's small lively pool were frozen, and the sere moss among the rocks was traced with flowers of frost. It was broad daylight, but the sun would not clear the mighty shoulder of the mountain for an hour yet: all western Gont, from sea-beaches to the peak, was sunless, silent, and clear in the winter morning. As the mage stood by the spring looking out over the falling lands and the harbor and the grey distances of the sea, wings beat above him. He looked up, raising one arm a little. A great hawk came down with loud-beating wings and lighted on his wrist. Like a trained hunting-bird it clung there, but it wore no broken leash, no band or bell. The claws dug hard in Ogion's wrist; the barred wings trembled; the round, gold eye was dull and wild.

"Are you messenger or message?" Ogion said gently to the hawk. "Come on with me—" As he spoke the hawk looked at him. Ogion was silent a minute. "I named you once, I think," he said, and then strode to his house and entered, bearing the bird still on his wrist. He made the hawk stand on the hearth in the fire's heat, and offered it water. It would not drink. Then Ogion began to lay a spell, very quietly, weaving the web of magic with his hands more than with words. When the spell was whole and woven he said softly,— "Ged,"— not looking at the falcon on the hearth. He waited some while, then turned, and got up, and went to the young man who stood trembling and dull-eyed before the fire.

Ged was richly and outlandishly dressed in fur and silk and silver, but the clothes were torn and stiff with sea-salt, and he stood gaunt and stooped, his hair lank about his scarred face.

Ogion took the soiled, princely cloak off his shoulders, led him to the alcove-room where his prentice once had slept and made him lie down on the pallet there, and so with a murmured sleep-charm left him. He had said no word to him, knowing that Ged had no human speech in him now.

As a boy, Ogion like all boys had thought it would be a very pleasant game to take by art-magic whatever shape one liked, man or beast, tree or cloud, and so to play at a thousand beings. But as a wizard he had learned the price of the game, which is the peril of losing one's self, playing away the truth. The longer a man stays in a form not his own, the greater this peril. Every prentice-sorcerer learns the tale of the wizard Bordger of Way, who delighted in taking bear's shape, and did so more and more often until the bear grew in him and the man died away, and he became a bear, and killed his own little son in the forests, and was hunted down and slain. And no one knows how many of the dolphins that leap in the waters of the Inmost Sea were men once, wise men, who forgot their wisdom and their name in the joy of the restless sea.

Ged had taken hawk-shape in fierce distress and rage, and when he flew from Osskil there had been but one thought in his mind: to outfly both Stone and shadow, to escape the cold treacherous lands, to go home. The falcon's anger and wildness were like his own, and had become his own, and his will to fly had become the falcon's will. Thus he had passed over Enlad, stooping down to drink at a lonely forest pool, but on the wing again at once, driven by fear of the shadow that came behind him. So he had crossed the great sea-lane called the Jaws of Enlad, and gone on and on, east by south, the hills of Oranéa faint to his right and the hills of Andrad fainter to his left, and before him only the sea; until at last, ahead, there rose up out of the waves one unchanging wave, towering always higher, the white peak of Gont. In all the sunlight and the dark of that great flight he had worn the falcon's wings, and looked through the falcon's eyes, and forgetting his own thoughts he had known at last only what the falcon knows: hunger, the wind, the way he flies.

He flew to the right haven. There were few on Roke and only one on Gont who could have made him back into a man.

He was savage and silent when he woke. Ogion never spoke to him, but gave him meat and water and let him sit hunched by the fire, grim as a great,

weary, sulking hawk. When night came he slept.
On the third morning he came in to the fireside
where the mage sat gazing at the flames, and said,
"Master . . ."

"Welcome, lad," said Ogion.

"I have come back to you as I left: a fool," the
young man said, his voice harsh and thickened.
The mage smiled a little and motioned Ged to sit
across the hearth from him, and set to brewing
them some tea.

Snow was falling, the first of the winter here on
the lower slopes of Gont. Ogion's windows were
shuttered fast, but they could hear the wet snow
as it fell soft on the roof, and the deep stillness of
snow all about the house. A long time they sat there
by the fire, and Ged told his old master the tale of
the years since he had sailed from Gont aboard the
ship called *Shadow*. Ogion asked no questions, and
when Ged was done he kept silent for a long time,
calm, pondering. Then he rose, and set out bread
and cheese and wine on the table, and they ate together. When they had done and had set the room
straight, Ogion spoke.

"Those are bitter scars you bear, lad," he said.

"I have no strength against the thing," Ged
answered.

Ogion shook his head but said no more for a

time. At length, "Strange," he said: "You had strength enough to outspell a sorcerer in his own domain, there in Osskil. You had strength enough to withstand the lures and fend off the attack of the servants of an Old Power of Earth. And at Pendor you had strength enough to stand up to a dragon."

"It was luck I had in Osskil, not strength," Ged replied, and he shivered again as he thought of the dreamlike deathly cold of the Court of the Terrenon. "As for the dragon, I knew his name. The evil thing, the shadow that hunts me, has no name."

"*All* things have a name," said Ogion, so certainly that Ged dared not repeat what the Archmage Gensher had told him, that such evil forces as he had loosed were nameless. The Dragon of Pendor, indeed, had offered to tell him the shadow's name, but he put little trust in the truth of that offer, nor did he believe Serret's promise that the Stone would tell him what he needed to know.

"If the shadow has a name," he said at last, "I do not think it will stop and tell it to me . . ."

"No," said Ogion. "Nor have you stopped and told it your name. And yet it knew it. On the moors in Osskil it called you by your name, the name I gave you. It is strange, strange . . ."

He fell to brooding again. At last Ged said, "I came here for counsel, not for refuge, Master. I will not bring this shadow upon you, and it will soon be here if I stay. Once you drove it from this very room—"

"No; that was but the foreboding of it, the shadow of a shadow. I could not drive it forth, now. Only you could do that."

"But I am powerless before it. Is there any place . . ." His voice died away before he had asked the question.

"There is no safe place," Ogion said gently. "Do not transform yourself again, Ged. The shadow seeks to destroy your true being. It nearly did so, driving you into hawk's being. No, where you should go, I do not know. Yet I have an idea of what you should do. It is a hard thing to say to you."

Ged's silence demanded truth, and Ogion said at last, "You must turn around."

"Turn around?"

"If you go ahead, if you keep running, wherever you run you will meet danger and evil, for it drives you, it chooses the way you go. You must choose. You must seek what seeks you. You must hunt the hunter."

Ged said nothing.

"At the spring of the River Ar I named you," the mage said, "a stream that falls from the mountain to the sea. A man would know the end he goes to, but he cannot know it if he does not turn, and return to his beginning, and hold that beginning in his being. If he would not be a stick whirled and whelmed in the stream, he must be the stream itself, all of it, from its spring to its sinking in the sea. You returned to Gont, you returned to me, Ged. Now turn clear round, and seek the very source, and that which lies before the source. There lies your hope of strength."

"There, Master?" Ged said with terror in his voice — "Where?"

Ogion did not answer.

"If I turn," Ged said after some time had gone by, "if as you say I hunt the hunter, I think the hunt will not be long. All its desire is to meet me face to face. And twice it has done so, and twice defeated me."

"Third time is the charm," said Ogion.

Ged paced the room up and down, from fireside to door, from door to fireside. "And if it defeats me wholly," he said, arguing perhaps with Ogion, perhaps with himself, "it will take my knowledge and my power, and use them. It threatens only me, now. But if it enters into me and possesses me, it will work great evil through me."

"That is true. If it defeats you."

"Yet if I run again, it will as surely find me again . . . And all my strength is spent in the running." Ged paced on a while, and then suddenly turned, and kneeling down before the mage he said, "I have walked with great wizards and have lived on the Isle of the Wise, but you are my true master, Ogion." He spoke with love, and with a somber joy.

"Good," said Ogion. "Now you know it. Better now than never. But you will be my master, in the end." He got up, and built up the fire to a good blaze, and hung the kettle over it to boil, and then pulling on his sheepskin coat said, "I must go look after my goats. Watch the kettle for me, lad."

When he came back in, all snow-powdered and stamping snow from his goatskin boots, he carried a long, rough shaft of yew-wood. All the end of the short afternoon, and again after their supper, he sat working by lampfire on the shaft with knife and rubbing-stone and spell-craft. Many times he passed his hands along the wood as if seeking any flaw. Often as he worked he sang softly. Ged, still weary, listened, and as he grew sleepy he thought himself a child in the witch's hut in Ten Alders village, on a snowy night in the firelit dark, the air heavy with herb-scent and smoke, and his mind all adrift on dreams as he listened to the long soft singing of spells and deeds of heroes who fought against dark powers and won, or lost, on distant islands long ago.

"There," said Ogion, and handed the finished staff to him. "The Archmage gave you yew-wood, a good choice and I kept to it. I meant the shaft for a long-bow, but it's better this way. Good night, my son."

As Ged, who found no words to thank him, turned away to his alcove-room, Ogion watched him and said, too soft for Ged to hear, "O my young falcon, fly well!"

In the cold dawn when Ogion woke, Ged was gone. Only he had left in wizardly fashion a message of silver-scrawled runes on the hearthstone, that faded even as Ogion read them: "Master, I go hunting."

# CHAPTER 8

# HUNTING

GED HAD SET OFF DOWN the road from Re Albi in the winter dark before sunrise, and before noon he came to the Port of Gont. Ogion had given him decent Gontish leggings and shirt and vest of leather and linen to replace his Osskilian finery, but Ged had kept for his winter journey the lordly cloak lined with pellawi-fur. So cloaked, empty-handed but for the dark staff that matched his height, he came to the Land Gate, and the soldiers lounging against the carven dragons there did not have to look twice at him to see the wizard. They drew aside their lances and let him enter without question, and watched him as he went on down the street.

On the quays and in the House of the Sea-Guild he asked of ships that might be going out north or west to Enlad, Andrad, Oranéa. All answered him that no ship would be leaving Gont Port now, so near Sunreturn, and at the Sea-Guild they told him that even fishingboats were not going out through the Armed Cliffs in the untrusty weather.

They offered him dinner at the buttery there in the Sea-Guild; a wizard seldom has to ask for his dinner. He sat a while with those longshoremen, shipwrights, and weatherworkers, taking pleasure in their slow, sparse conversation, their grumbling Gontish speech. There was a great wish in him to stay here on Gont, and forgoing all wizardry and venture, forgetting all power and horror, to live in peace like any man on the known, dear ground of his home land. That was his wish; but his will was other. He did not stay long in the Sea-Guild, nor in the city, after he found there would be no ships out of port. He set out walking along the bay shore till he came to the first of the small villages that lie north of the City of Gont, and there he asked among the fishermen till he found one that had a boat to sell.

The fisherman was a dour old man. His boat, twelve foot long and clinker-built, was so warped and sprung as to be scarce seaworthy, yet he asked a high price for her: the spell of sea-safety for a year laid on his own boat, himself, and his son. For Gontish fishermen fear nothing, not even wizards, only the sea.

That spell of sea-safety which they set much

store by in the Northern Archipelago never saved
a man from storm-wind or storm-wave, but, cast
by one who knows the local seas and the ways of a
boat and the skills of the sailor, it weaves some daily safety about the fisherman. Ged made the charm
well and honestly, working on it all that night and
the next day, omitting nothing, sure and patient,
though all the while his mind was strained with
fear and his thoughts went on dark paths seeking
to imagine how the shadow would appear to him
next, and how soon, and where. When the spell
was made whole and cast, he was very weary. He
slept that night in the fisherman's hut in a whale-
gut hammock, and got up at dawn smelling like a
dried herring, and went down to the cove under
Cutnorth Cliff where his new boat lay.

He pushed it into the quiet water by the landing,
and water began to well softly into it at once. Stepping into the boat light as a cat Ged set straight the
warped boards and rotten pegs, working both with
tools and incantations, as he had used to do with
Pechvarry in Low Torning. The people of the village gathered in silence, not too close, to watch his
quick hands and listen to his soft voice. This job
too he did well and patiently until it was done and
the boat was sealed and sound. Then he set up his
staff that Ogion had made him for a mast, stayed
it with spells, and fixed across it a yard of sound

wood. Downward from this yard he wove on the wind's loom a sail of spells, a square sail white as the snows on Gont peak above. At this the women watching sighed with envy. Then standing by the mast Ged raised up the magewind lightly. The boat moved out upon the water, turning towards the Armed Cliffs across the great bay. When the silent watching fishermen saw that leaky rowboat slip out under sail as quick and neat as a sandpiper taking wing, then they raised a cheer, grinning and stamping in the cold wind on the beach; and Ged looking back a moment saw them there cheering him on, under the dark jagged bulk of Cutnorth Cliff, above which the snowy fields of the Mountain rose up into cloud.

He sailed across the bay and out between the Armed Cliffs onto the Gontish Sea, there setting his course northwestwards to pass north of Oranéa, returning as he had come. He had no plan or strategy in this but the retracing of his course. Following his falcon-flight across the days and winds from Osskil, the shadow might wander or might come straight, there was no telling. But unless it had withdrawn again wholly into the dream-realm, it should not miss Ged coming openly, over open sea, to meet it.

On the sea he wished to meet it, if meet it must. He was not sure why this was, yet he had a terror of meeting the thing again on dry land. Out of the sea there rise storms and monsters, but no evil powers: evil is of earth. And there is no sea, no running of river or spring, in the dark land where once Ged had gone. Death is the dry place. Though the sea itself was a danger to him in the hard weather of the season, that danger and change and instability seemed to him a defense and chance. And when he met the shadow in this final end of his folly, he thought, maybe at least he could grip the thing even as it gripped him, and drag it with the weight of his body and the weight of his own death down into the darkness of the deep sea, from which, so held, it might not rise again. So at least his death would put an end to the evil he had loosed by living.

He sailed a rough chopping sea above which clouds drooped and drifted in vast mournful veils. He raised no magewind now but used the world's wind, which blew keen from the northwest; and so long as he maintained the substance of his spell-woven sail often with a whispered word, the sail itself set and turned itself to catch the wind. Had he not used that magic he would have been hard put to keep the crank little boat on such a course, on that rough sea. On he went, and kept keen lookout on all sides. The fisherman's wife had given him two loaves of bread and a jar of water, and after some hours, when he was first in sight of Kameber Rock, the only isle between Gont and Oranéa, he ate and drank, and thought gratefully of the silent Gontishwoman who had given him the food. On past the dim glimpse of land he sailed, tacking more westerly now, in a faint dank drizzle that over land might be a light snow. There was no sound at all but the small creaking of the boat and light slap of waves on her bow. No boat or bird went by. Nothing moved but the ever-moving water and the drifting clouds, the clouds that he remembered dimly as flowing all about him as he, a falcon, flew east on this same course he now followed to the west; and he had looked down on the grey sea then as now he looked up at the grey air.

Nothing was ahead when he looked around. He stood up, chilled, weary of this gazing and peering into empty murk. "Come then," he muttered, "come on, what do you wait for, Shadow?" There was no answer, no darker motion among the dark mists and waves. Yet he knew more and more surely now that the thing was not far off, seeking blindly down his cold trail. And all at once he shouted out aloud, "I am here, I Ged the Sparrowhawk, and I summon my shadow!"

The boat creaked, the waves lisped, the wind hissed a little on the white sail. The moments went by. Still Ged waited, one hand on the yew-wood

mast of his boat, staring into the icy drizzle that
slowly drove in ragged lines across the sea from the
north. The moments went by. Then, far off in the
rain over the water, he saw the shadow coming.

It had done with the body of the Osskilian oarsman Skiorh, and not as gebbeth did it follow him
through the winds and over sea. Nor did it wear
that beast-shape in which he had seen it on Roke
Knoll, and in his dreams. Yet it had a shape now,
even in the daylight. In its pursuit of Ged and in
its struggle with him on the moors it had drawn
power from him, sucking it into itself: and it may
be that his summoning of it, aloud in the light of
day, had given to it or forced upon it some form
and semblance. Certainly it had now some likeness
to a man, though being shadow it cast no shadow.
So it came over the sea, out of the Jaws of Enlad
towards Gont, a dim ill-made thing pacing uneasy
on the waves, peering down the wind as it came;
and the cold rain blew through it.

Because it was half blinded by the day, and because he had called it, Ged saw it before it saw him.
He knew it, as it knew him, among all beings, all
shadows.

In the terrible solitude of the winter sea Ged
stood and saw the thing he feared. The wind
seemed to blow it farther from the boat, and the
waves ran under it bewildering his eye, and ever

and again it seemed closer to him. He could not tell if it moved or not. It had seen him, now. Though there was nothing in his mind but horror and fear of its touch, the cold black pain that drained his life away, yet he waited, unmoving. Then all at once speaking aloud he called the magewind strong and sudden into his white sail, and his boat leapt across the grey waves straight at the lowering thing that hung upon the wind.

In utter silence the shadow, wavering, turned and fled.

Upwind it went, northward. Upwind Ged's boat followed, shadow-speed against mage-craft, the rainy gale against them both. And the young man yelled to his boat, to the sail and the wind and the waves ahead, as a hunter yells to his hounds when the wolf runs in plain sight before them, and he brought into that spell-woven sail a wind that would have split any sail of cloth and that drove his boat over the sea like a scud of blown foam, closer always to the thing that fled.

Now the shadow turned, making a half-circle, and appearing all at once more loose and dim, less like a man, more like mere smoke blowing on the wind, it doubled back and ran downwind with the gale, as if it made for Gont.

With hand and spell Ged turned his boat, and it leaped like a dolphin from the water, rolling, in that quick turn. Faster than before he followed, but the shadow grew ever fainter to his eyes. Rain, mixed with sleet and snow, came stinging across his back and his left cheek, and he could not see more than a hundred yards ahead. Before long, as the storm grew heavier, the shadow was lost to sight. Yet Ged was sure of its track as if he followed a beast's track over snow, instead of a wraith fleeing over water. Though the wind blew his way now he held the singing magewind in the sail, and flake-foam shot from the boat's blunt prow, and she slapped the water as she went.

For a long time hunted and hunter held their weird, fleet course, and the day was darkening fast. Ged knew that at the great pace he had gone these past hours he must be south of Gont, heading past it towards Spevy or Torheven, or even past these islands out into the open Reach. He could not tell. He did not care. He hunted, he followed, and fear ran before him.

All at once he saw the shadow for a moment not far from him. The world's wind had been sinking, and the driving sleet of the storm had given way to a chill, ragged, thickening mist. Through this mist he glimpsed the shadow, fleeing somewhat to the right of his course. He spoke to wind and sail and turned the tiller and pursued, though again it was a blind pursuit: the fog thickened fast, boiling and

tattering where it met with the spellwind, closing
down all round the boat, a featureless pallor that
deadened light and sight. Even as Ged spoke the
first word of a clearing-charm, he saw the shadow
again, still to the right of his course but very near,
and going slowly. The fog blew through the faceless vagueness of its head, yet it was shaped like
a man, only deformed and changing, like a man's
shadow. Ged veered the boat once more, thinking
he had run his enemy to ground: in that instant
it vanished, and it was his boat that ran aground,
smashing up on shoal rocks that the blowing mist
had hidden from his sight. He was pitched nearly
out, but grabbed hold on the mast-staff before the
next breaker struck. This was a great wave, which
threw the little boat up out of water and brought
her down on a rock, as a man might lift up and
crush a snail's shell.

Stout and wizardly was the staff Ogion had
shaped. It did not break, and buoyant as a dry log
it rode the water. Still grasping it Ged was pulled
back as the breakers streamed back from the shoal,
so that he was in deep water and saved, till the next
wave, from battering on the rocks. Salt-blinded and
choked, he tried to keep his head up and to fight
the enormous pull of the sea. There was sand beach
a little aside of the rocks, he glimpsed this a couple
of times as he tried to swim free of the rising of the

next breaker. With all his strength and with the staff's power aiding him he struggled to make for that beach. He got no nearer. The surge and recoil of the swells tossed him back and forth like a rag, and the cold of the deep sea drew warmth fast from his body, weakening him till he could not move his arms. He had lost sight of rocks and beach alike, and did not know what way he faced. There was only a tumult of water around him, under him, over him, blinding him, strangling him, drowning him.

A wave swelling in under the ragged fog took him and rolled him over and over and flung him up like a stick of driftwood on the sand.

There he lay. He still clutched the yew-wood staff with both hands. Lesser waves dragged at him, trying to tug him back down the sand in their out-going rush, and the mist parted and closed above him, and later a sleety rain beat on him.

After a long time he moved. He got up on hands and knees, and began slowly crawling up the beach, away from the water's edge. It was black night now, but he whispered to the staff, and a little werelight clung about it. With this to guide him he struggled forward, little by little, up toward the dunes. He was so beaten and broken and cold that this crawling through the wet sand in the whistling, sea-thundering dark was the hardest thing he had ever had to do. And once or twice it seemed to him that the great noise of the sea and the wind all died away and the wet sand turned to dust under his hands, and he felt the unmoving gaze of strange stars on his back: but he did not lift his head, and he crawled on, and after a while he heard his own gasping breath, and felt the bitter wind beat the rain against his face.

The moving brought a little warmth back into him at last, and after he had crept up into the dunes, where the gusts of rainy wind came less hard, he managed to get up on his feet. He spoke a stronger light out of the staff, for the world was utterly black, and then leaning on the staff he went on, stumbling and halting, half a mile or so inland. Then on the rise of a dune he heard the sea, louder again, not behind him but in front: the dunes sloped down again to another shore. This was no island he was on but a mere reef, a bit of sand in the midst of the ocean.

He was too worn out to despair, but he gave a kind of sob and stood there, bewildered, leaning on his staff, for a long time. Then doggedly he turned to the left, so the wind would be at his back at least, and shuffled down the high dune, seeking some hollow among the ice-rimed, bowing seagrass where he could have a little shelter. As he held up the staff to see what lay before him, he caught a dull gleam at the farthest edge of the circle of werelight: a wall of rain-wet wood.

It was a hut or shed, small and rickety as if a child had built it. Ged knocked on the low door with his staff. It remained shut. Ged pushed it open and entered, stooping nearly double to do so. He could not stand up straight inside the hut. Coals lay red in the firepit, and by their dim glow Ged saw a man with white, long hair, who crouched in terror against the far wall, and another, man or woman he could not tell, peering from a heap of rags or hides on the floor.

"I won't hurt you," Ged whispered.

They said nothing. He looked from one to the other. Their eyes were blank with terror. When he laid down his staff, the one under the pile of rags hid whimpering. Ged took off his cloak that was heavy with water and ice, stripped naked and huddled over the firepit. "Give me something to wrap myself in," he said. He was hoarse, and could hardly speak for the chattering of his teeth and the long shudders that shook him. If they heard him, neither of the old ones answered. He reached out and took a rag from the bed-heap—a goat-hide, it might have been years ago, but it was now all tatters and black grease. The one under the bed-heap moaned with fear, but Ged paid no heed. He rubbed himself dry and then whispered, "Have you wood? Build up the fire a little, old man. I come to you in need, I mean you no harm."

The old man did not move, watching him in a stupor of fear.

"Do you understand me? Do you speak no Hardic?" Ged paused, and then asked, "Kargad?"

At that word, the old man nodded all at once, one nod, like a sad old puppet on strings. But as it was the only word Ged knew of the Kargish language, it was the end of their conversation. He found wood piled by one wall, built up the fire himself, and then with gestures asked for water, for swallowing sea-water had sickened him and now he was parched with thirst. Cringing, the old man pointed to a great shell that held water, and pushed towards the fire another shell in which were strips of smoke-dried fish. So, cross-legged close by the fire, Ged drank, and ate a little, and as some strength and sense began to come back into him, he wondered where he was. Even with the magewind he could not have sailed clear to the Kargad Lands. This islet must be out in the Reach, east of Gont but still west of Karego-At. It seemed strange that people dwelt on so small and forlorn a place, a mere sandbar; maybe they were castaways; but he was too weary to puzzle his head about them then.

He kept turning his cloak to the heat. The silvery pellawi-fur dried fast, and as soon as the wool of the facing was at least warm, if not dry, he wrapped himself in it and stretched out by the firepit. "Go to sleep, poor folk," he said to his silent hosts, and laid his head down on the floor of sand, and slept.

Three nights he spent on the nameless isle, for the first morning when he woke he was sore in every muscle and feverish and sick. He lay like a log of driftwood in the hut by the firepit all that day and night. The next morning he woke still stiff and sore, but recovered. He put back on his salt-crusted clothes, for there was not enough water to wash them, and going out into the grey windy morning looked over this place whereto the shadow had tricked him.

It was a rocky sandbar a mile wide at its widest and a little longer than that, fringed all about with shoals and rocks. No tree or bush grew on it, no plant but the bowing sea-grass. The hut stood in a hollow of the dunes, and the old man and woman lived there alone in the utter desolation of the empty sea. The hut was built, or piled up rather, of driftwood planks and branches. Their water came from a little brackish well beside the hut; their food was fish and shellfish, fresh or dried, and rockweed. The tattered hides in the hut, and a little store of bone needles and fishhooks, and the sinew for fish-lines and firedrill, came not from goats as Ged had thought at first, but from spotted seal; and indeed this was the kind of place where the seal will go to raise their pups in summer. But no one else comes to such a place. The old ones feared Ged not because they thought him a spirit, and not because he was a wizard, but only because he was a man. They had forgotten that there were other people in the world.

The old man's sullen dread never lessened. When he thought Ged was coming close enough to touch him, he would hobble away, peering back with a scowl around his bush of dirty white hair. At first the old woman had whimpered and hidden under her rag-pile whenever Ged moved, but as he had lain dozing feverishly in the dark hut, he saw her squatting to stare at him with a strange, dull, yearning look; and after a while she had brought him water to drink. When he sat up to take the shell from her she was scared and dropped it, spilling all the water, and then she wept, and wiped her eyes with her long whitish-grey hair.

Now she watched him as he worked down on the beach, shaping driftwood and planks from his boat that had washed ashore into a new boat, using the old man's crude stone adze and a binding-spell. This was neither a repair nor a boat-building, for he had not enough proper wood, and must supply all his wants with pure wizardry. Yet the old woman did not watch his marvelous work so much as she watched him, with that same craving look in her eyes. After a while she went off, and came back presently with a gift: a handful of mussels she had gathered on the rocks. Ged ate them as she gave them to him, sea-wet and raw, and thanked her. Seeming to gain courage, she went to the hut and came back with something again in her hands, a bundle wrapped up in a rag. Timidly, watching his face all the while, she unwrapped the thing and held it up for him to see.

It was a little child's dress of silk brocade stiff with seed-pearls, stained with salt, yellow with years. On the small bodice the pearls were worked in a shape Ged knew: the double arrow of the God-Brothers of the Kargad Empire, surmounted by a king's crown.

The old woman, wrinkled, dirty, clothed in an ill-sewn sack of sealskin, pointed at the little silken dress and at herself, and smiled: a sweet, unmeaning smile, like a baby's. From some hidingplace sewn in the skirt of the dress she took a small object, and this was held out to Ged. It was a bit of dark metal, a piece of broken jewelry perhaps, the half-circle of a broken ring. Ged looked at it, but she gestured that he take it, and was not satisfied until he took it; then she nodded and smiled again; she had made him a present. But the dress she wrapped up carefully in its greasy rag-coverings, and she shuffled back to the hut to hide the lovely thing away.

Ged put the broken ring into his tunic-pocket with almost the same care, for his heart was full of pity. He guessed now that these two might be children of some royal house of the Kargad Empire; a tyrant or usurper who feared to shed kingly blood had sent them to be cast away, to live or die, on an uncharted islet far from Karego-At. One had been a boy of eight or ten, maybe, and the other a stout baby princess in a dress of silk and pearls; and they had lived, and lived on alone, forty years, fifty years, on a rock in the ocean, prince and princess of Desolation.

But the truth of this guess he did not learn until, years later, the quest of the Ring of Erreth-Akbe led him to the Kargad Lands, and to the Tombs of Atuan.

His third night on the isle lightened to a calm, pale sunrise. It was the day of Sunreturn, the shortest day of the year. His little boat of wood and magic, scraps and spells, was ready. He had tried to tell the old ones that he would take them to any land, Gont or Spevy or the Torikles; he would have left them even on some lonely shore of Karego-At, had they asked it of him, though Kargish waters were no safe place for an Archipelagan to venture.

But they would not leave their barren isle. The old woman seemed not to understand what he meant with his gestures and quiet words; the old man did understand, and refused. All his memory of other lands and other men was a child's nightmare of blood and giants and screaming: Ged could see that in his face, as he shook his head and shook his head.

So Ged that morning filled up a sealskin pouch with water at the well, and since he could not thank the old ones for their fire and food, and had no present for the old woman as he would have liked, he did what he could, and set a charm on that salty unreliable spring. The water rose up through the sand as sweet and clear as any mountain spring in the heights of Gont, nor did it ever fail. Because of it, that place of dunes and rocks is charted now and bears a name; sailors call it Springwater Isle. But the hut is gone, and the storms of many winters have left no sign of the two who lived out their lives there and died alone.

They kept hidden in the hut, as if they feared to watch, when Ged ran his boat out from the sandy south end of the isle. He let the world's wind, steady from the north, fill his sail of spell-cloth, and went speedily forth over the sea.

Now this sea-quest of Ged's was a strange matter, for as he well knew, he was a hunter who knew neither what the thing was that he hunted, nor where in all Earthsea it might be. He must hunt it by guess, by hunch, by luck, even as it had hunted him. Each was blind to the other's being, Ged as baffled by impalpable shadows as the shadow was baffled by daylight and by solid things. One certainty only Ged had: that he was indeed the hunter now and not the hunted. For the shadow, having tricked him onto the rocks, might have had him at its mercy all the while he lay half-dead on the shore and blundered in darkness in the stormy dunes; but it had not waited for that chance. It had tricked him and fled away at once, not daring now to face him. In this he saw that Ogion had been right: the shadow could not draw on his power, so long as he was turned against it. So he must keep against it, keep after it, though its track was cold across these wide seas, and he had nothing at all to guide him but the luck of the world's wind blowing southward, and a dim guess or notion in his mind that south or east was the right way to follow.

Before nightfall he saw away off on his left hand the long, faint shoreline of a great land, which must be Karego-At. He was in the very sea-roads of those white barbaric folk. He kept a sharp watch out for any Kargish longship or galley; and he remembered, as he sailed through red evening, that morning of his boyhood in Ten Alders village, the plumed warriors, the fire, the mist. And thinking of that day he saw all at once, with a qualm at his heart, how the shadow had tricked him with his own trick, bringing that mist about him on the sea as if bringing it out of his own past, blinding him to danger and fooling him to his death.

He kept his course to the southeast, and the land sank out of sight as night came over the eastern edge of the world. The hollows of the waves all were full of darkness while the crests shone yet with a clear ruddy reflection of the west. Ged sang aloud the Winter Carol, and such cantos of the *Deed of the Young King* as he remembered, for those songs are sung at the Festival of Sunreturn. His voice was clear, but it fell to nothing in the vast silence of the sea. Darkness came quickly, and the winter stars.

All that longest night of the year he waked, watching the stars rise upon his left hand and wheel overhead and sink into far black waters on the right, while always the long wind of winter bore him southward over an unseen sea. He could sleep for only a moment now and then, with a sharp awakening. This boat he sailed was in truth no boat but a thing more than half charm and sorcery, and the rest of it mere planks and driftwood which, if he let slack the shaping-spells and the binding-spell upon them, would soon enough lapse and scatter and go drifting off as a little flotsam on the waves. The sail

too, woven of magic and the air, would not long
stay against the wind if he slept, but would turn to
a puff of wind itself. Ged's spells were cogent and
potent, but when the matter on which such spells
works is small, the power that keeps them working must be renewed from moment to moment: so
he slept not that night. He would have gone easier
and swifter as falcon or dolphin, but Ogion had
advised him not to change his shape, and he knew
the value of Ogion's advice. So he sailed southward
under the west-going stars, and the long night
passed slowly, until the first day of the new year
brightened all the sea.

Soon after the sun rose he saw land ahead, but
he was making little way towards it. The world's
wind had dropped with daybreak. He raised a light
magewind into his sail, to drive him towards that
land. At the sight of it, fear had come into him
again, the sinking dread that urged him to turn
away, to run away. And he followed that fear as a
hunter follows the signs, the broad, blunt, clawed
tracks of the bear, that may at any moment turn on
him from the thickets. For he was close now: he
knew it.

It was a queer-looking land that loomed up
over the sea as he drew nearer and nearer. What
had from afar seemed to be one sheer mountain-
wall was split into several long steep ridges, sepa-

rate isles perhaps, between which the sea ran in narrow sounds or channels. Ged had pored over many charts and maps in the Tower of the Master Namer on Roke, but those had been mostly of the Archipelago and the inner seas. He was out in the East Reach now, and did not know what this island might be. Nor had he much thought for that. It was fear that lay ahead of him, that lurked hiding from him or waiting for him among the slopes and forests of the island, and straight for it he steered.

Now the dark forest-crowned cliffs gloomed and towered high over his boat, and spray from the waves that broke against the rocky headlands blew spattering against his sail, as the magewind bore him between two great capes into a sound, a sea-lane that ran on before him deep into the island, no wider than the length of two galleys. The sea, confined, was restless and fretted at the steep shores. There were no beaches, for the cliffs dropped straight down into the water that lay darkened by the cold reflection of their heights. It was windless, and very silent.

The shadow had tricked him out onto the moors in Osskil, and tricked him in the mist onto the rocks, and now would there be a third trick? Had he driven the thing here, or had it drawn him here, into a trap? He did not know. He knew only the torment of dread, and the certainty that he must go

ahead and do what he had set out to do: hunt down
the evil, follow his terror to its source. Very cau-
tiously he steered, watching before him and behind
him and up and down the cliffs on either hand. He
had left the sunlight of the new day behind him
on the open sea. All was dark here. The opening
between the headlands seemed a remote, bright
gateway when he glanced back. The cliffs loomed
higher and ever higher overhead as he approached
the mountain-root from which they sprang, and
the lane of water grew narrower. He peered ahead
into the dark cleft, and left and right up the great,
cavern-pocked, boulder-tumbled slopes where
trees crouched with their roots half in air. Nothing moved. Now he was coming to the end of the
inlet, a high blank wrinkled mass of rock against
which, narrowed to the width of a little creek, the
last sea-waves lapped feebly. Fallen boulders and
rotten trunks and the roots of gnarled trees left
only a tight way to steer. A trap: a dark trap under
the roots of the silent mountain, and he was in the
trap. Nothing moved before him or above him. All
was deathly still. He could go no further.

He turned the boat around, working her carefully round with spell and with makeshift oar lest
she knock up against the underwater rocks or be
entangled in the outreaching roots and branches,
till she faced outward again; and he was about to

raise up a wind to take him back as he had come, when suddenly the words of the spell froze on his lips, and his heart went cold within him. He looked back over his shoulder. The shadow stood behind him in the boat.

Had he lost one instant, he had been lost; but he was ready, and lunged to seize and hold the thing which wavered and trembled there within arm's reach. No wizardry would serve him now, but only his own flesh, his life itself, against the unliving. He spoke no word, but attacked, and the boat plunged and pitched from his sudden turn and lunge. And a pain ran up his arms into his breast, taking away his breath, and an icy cold filled him, and he was blinded: yet in his hands that seized the shadow there was nothing—darkness, air.

He stumbled forward, catching the mast to stay his fall, and light came shooting back into his eyes. He saw the shadow shudder away from him and shrink together, then stretch hugely up over him, over the sail, for an instant. Then like black smoke on the wind it recoiled and fled, formless, down the water towards the bright gate between the cliffs.

Ged sank to his knees. The little spell-patched boat pitched again, rocked itself to stillness, drifting on the uneasy waves. He crouched in it, numb, unthinking, struggling to draw breath, until at last

cold water welling under his hands warned him
that he must see to his boat, for the spells binding it
were growing weak. He stood up, holding on to the
staff that made the mast, and rewove the binding-
spell as best he could. He was chilled and weary;
his hands and arms ached sorely, and there was no
power in him. He wished he might lie down there
in that dark place where sea and mountain met and
sleep, sleep on the restless rocking water.

He could not tell if this weariness were a sorcery
laid on him by the shadow as it fled, or came of
the bitter coldness of its touch, or was from mere
hunger and want of sleep and expense of strength;
but he struggled against it, forcing himself to raise
up a light magewind into the sail and follow down
the dark seaway where the shadow had fled.

All terror was gone. All joy was gone. It was a
chase no longer. He was neither hunted nor hunter,
now. For the third time they had met and touched:
he had of his own will turned to the shadow, seeking to hold it with living hands. He had not held
it, but he had forged between them a bond, a link
that had no breaking-point. There was no need
to hunt the thing down, to track it, nor would its
flight avail it. Neither could escape. When they
had come to the time and place for their last meeting, they would meet.

But until that time, and elsewhere than that place, there would never be any rest or peace for Ged, day or night, on earth or sea. He knew now, and the knowledge was hard, that his task had never been to undo what he had done, but to finish what he had begun.

He sailed out from between the dark cliffs, and on the sea was broad, bright morning, with a fair wind blowing from the north.

He drank what water he had left in the seal-skin pouch, and steered around the westernmost headland until he came into a wide strait between it and a second island lying to the west. Then he knew the place, calling to mind sea-charts of the East Reach. These were the Hands, a pair of lonely isles that reach their mountain-fingers northward toward the Kargad Lands. He sailed on between the two, and as the afternoon darkened with storm-clouds coming up from the north he came to shore, on the southern coast of the west isle. He had seen there was a little village there, above the beach where a stream came tumbling down to the sea, and he cared little what welcome he got if he could have water, fire's warmth, and sleep.

The villagers were rough shy people, awed by a wizard's staff, wary of a strange face, but hospitable to one who came alone, over sea, before a storm.

They gave him meat and drink in plenty, and the comfort of firelight and the comfort of human voices speaking his own Hardic tongue, and last and best they gave him hot water to wash the cold and saltness of the sea from him, and a bed where he could sleep.

# CHAPTER 9

# IFFISH

**GED SPENT THREE DAYS IN** that village of the West Hand, recovering himself, and making ready a boat built not of spells and sea-wrack but of sound wood well pegged and caulked, with a stout mast and sail of her own, that he might sail easily and sleep when he needed. Like most boats of the North and the Reaches she was clinker-built, with planks overlapped and clenched one upon the other for strength in the high seas; every part of her was sturdy and well-made. Ged reinforced her wood with deep-in-woven charms, for he thought he might go far in that boat. She was built to carry two or three men, and the old man who owned her said that he and his brothers had been through high seas and foul weather with her and she had ridden all gallantly.

Unlike the shrewd fisherman of Gont, this old man, for fear and wonder of his wizardry, would have given the boat to Ged. But Ged paid him for it in sorcerers' kind, healing his eyes of the cataracts that were in the way of blinding him. Then the old man, rejoicing, said to him, "We called the boat *Sanderling,* but do you call her *Lookfar,* and paint eyes aside her prow, and my thanks will look out of that blind wood for you and keep you from rock and reef. For I had forgotten how much light there is in the world, till you gave it back to me."

Other works Ged also did in his days in that village under the steep forests of the Hand, as his power came back into him. These were such people as he had known as a boy in the Northward Vale of Gont, though poorer even than those. With them he was at home, as he would never be in the courts of the wealthy, and he knew their bitter wants without having to ask. So he laid charms of heal and ward on children who were lame or sickly, and spells of increase on the villagers' scrawny flocks of goats and sheep; he set the rune Simn on the spindles and looms, the boat's oars and tools of bronze and stone they brought him, that these might do their work well; and the rune Pirr he wrote on the rooftrees of the huts, which protects the house and its folk from fire, wind, and madness.

When his boat *Lookfar* was ready and well stocked with water and dried fish, he stayed yet one more day in the village, to teach to their young chanter the *Deed of Morred* and the Havnorian Lay. Very seldom did any Archipelagan ship touch at

the Hands: songs made a hundred years ago were
news to those villagers, and they craved to hear of
heroes. Had Ged been free of what was laid on
him he would gladly have stayed there a week or a
month to sing them what he knew, that the great
songs might be known on a new isle. But he was
not free, and the next morning he set sail, going
straight south over the wide seas of the Reach. For
southward the shadow had gone. He need cast no
finding-charm to know this: he knew it, as certainly as if a fine unreeling cord bound him and it
together, no matter what miles and seas and lands
might lie between. So he went certain, unhurried,
and unhopeful on the way he must go, and the
wind of winter bore him to the south.

He sailed a day and a night over the lonesome
sea, and on the second day he came to a small isle,
which they told him was called Vemish. The people in the little port looked at him askance, and
soon their sorcerer came hurrying. He looked hard
at Ged, and then he bowed, and said in a voice that
was both pompous and wheedling, "Lord Wizard!
forgive my temerity, and honor us by accepting of
us anything you may need for your voyage—food,
drink, sailcloth, rope,—my daughter is fetching to
your boat at this moment a brace of fresh-roasted
hens—I think it prudent, however, that you con-
tinue on your way from here as soon as it meets

your convenience to do so. The people are in some dismay. For not long ago, the day before yesterday, a person was seen crossing our humble isle afoot from north to south, and no boat was seen to come with him aboard it nor no boat was seen to leave with him aboard it, and it did not seem that he cast any shadow. Those who saw this person tell me that he bore some likeness to yourself."

At that, Ged bowed his own head, and turned and went back to the docks of Vemish and sailed out, not looking back. There was no profit in frightening the islanders or making an enemy of their sorcerer. He would rather sleep at sea again, and think over this news the sorcerer had told him, for he was sorely puzzled by it.

The day ended, and the night passed with cold rain whispering over the sea all through the dark hours, and a grey dawn. Still the mild north wind carried *Lookfar* on. After noon the rain and mist blew off, and the sun shone from time to time; and late in the day Ged saw right athwart his course the low blue hills of a great island, brightened by that drifting winter sunlight. The smoke of hearth-fires lingered blue over the slate roofs of little towns among those hills, a pleasant sight in the vast sameness of the sea.

Ged followed a fishing-fleet in to their port, and going up the streets of the town in the golden win-

ter evening he found an inn called The Harrekki,
where firelight and ale and roast ribs of mutton
warmed him body and soul. At the tables of the
inn there were a couple of other voyagers, traders
of the East Reach, but most of the men were townsfolk come there for good ale, news, and conversation. They were not rough timid people like the
fisher-folk of the Hands, but true townsmen, alert
and sedate. Surely they knew Ged for a wizard,
but nothing at all was said of it, except that the
innkeeper in talking (and he was a talkative man)
mentioned that this town, Ismay, was fortunate in
sharing with other towns of the island the inesti-
mable treasure of an accomplished wizard trained
at the School on Roke, who had been given his
staff by the Archmage himself, and who, though
out of town at the moment, dwelt in his ancestral
home right in Ismay itself, which, therefore, stood
in no need of any other practitioner of the High
Arts. "As they say, *two staffs in one town must come
to blows,* isn't it so, Sir?" said the innkeeper, smiling and full of cheer. So Ged was informed that as
journeyman-wizard, one seeking a livelihood from
sorcery, he was not wanted here. Thus he had got a
blunt dismissal from Vemish and a bland one from
Ismay, and he wondered at what he had been told
about the kindly ways of the East Reach. This isle
was Iffish, where his friend Vetch had been born.

It did not seem so hospitable a place as Vetch had said.

And yet he saw that they were, indeed, kindly faces enough. It was only that they sensed what he knew to be true: that he was set apart from them, cut off from them, that he bore a doom upon him and followed after a dark thing. He was like a cold wind blowing through the firelit room, like a black bird carried by on a storm from foreign lands. The sooner he went on, taking his evil destiny with him, the better for these folk.

"I am on quest," he said to the innkeeper. "I will be here only a night or two." His tone was bleak. The innkeeper, with a glance at the great yew-staff in the corner, said nothing at all for once, but filled up Ged's cup with brown ale till the foam ran over the top.

Ged knew that he should spend only the one night in Ismay. There was no welcome for him there, or anywhere. He must go where he was bound. But he was sick of the cold empty sea and the silence where no voice spoke to him. He told himself he would spend one day in Ismay, and on the morrow go. So he slept late; when he woke a light snow was falling, and he idled about the lanes and byways of the town to watch the people busy at their doings. He watched children bundled in fur capes playing at snow-castle and building snow-

men; he heard gossips chatting across the street
from open doors, and watched the bronze-smith
at work with a little lad red-faced and sweating to
pump the long bellows-sleeves at the smelting pit;
through windows lit with a dim ruddy gold from
within as the short day darkened he saw women at
their looms, turning a moment to speak or smile to
child or husband there in the warmth within the
house. Ged saw all these things from outside and
apart, alone, and his heart was very heavy in him,
though he would not admit to himself that he was
sad. As night fell he still lingered in the streets, re-
luctant to go back to the inn. He heard a man and
a girl talking together merrily as they came down
the street past him towards the town square, and
all at once he turned, for he knew the man's voice.

He followed and caught up with the pair, coming up beside them in the late twilight lit only by
distant lantern-gleams. The girl stepped back, but
the man stared at him and then flung up the staff
he carried, holding it between them as a barrier
to ward off the threat or act of evil. And that was
somewhat more than Ged could bear. His voice
shook a little as he said, "I thought you would
know me, Vetch."

Even then Vetch hesitated for a moment.

"I do know you," he said, and lowered the staff
and took Ged's hand and hugged him round the

shoulders—"I do know you! Welcome, my friend, welcome! What a sorry greeting I gave you, as if you were a ghost coming up from behind—and I have waited for you to come, and looked for you—"

"So you are the wizard they boast of in Ismay? I wondered—"

"Oh, yes, I'm their wizard; but listen, let me tell you why I didn't know you, lad. Maybe I've looked too hard for you. Three days ago—were you here three days ago, on Iffish?"

"I came yesterday."

"Three days ago, in the street in Quor, the village up there in the hills, I saw you. That is, I saw a presentment of you, or an imitation of you, or maybe simply a man who looks like you. He was ahead of me, going out of town, and he turned a bend in the road even as I saw him. I called and got no answer, I followed and found no one; nor any tracks; but the ground was frozen. It was a queer thing, and now seeing you come up out of the shadows like that I thought I was tricked again. I am sorry, Ged!" He spoke Ged's true name softly, so that the girl who stood waiting a little way behind him would not hear it.

Ged also spoke low, to use his friend's true name: "No matter, Estarriol. But this is myself, and I am glad to see you . . ."

Vetch heard, perhaps, something more than

simple gladness in his voice. He had not yet let go
of Ged's shoulder, and he said now, in the True
Speech, "In trouble and from darkness you come,
Ged, yet your coming is joy to me." Then he went
on in his Reach-accented Hardic, "Come on, come
home with us, we're going home, it's time to get in
out of the dark!—This is my sister, the youngest
of us, prettier than I am as you see, but much less
clever: Yarrow she's called. Yarrow, this is the Sparrowhawk, the best of us and my friend."

"Lord Wizard," the girl greeted him, and deco-
rously she bobbed her head and hid her eyes with
her hands to show respect, as women did in the
East Reach; her eyes when not hidden were clear,
shy, and curious. She was perhaps fourteen years
old, dark like her brother, but very slight and slender. On her sleeve there clung, winged and taloned,
a dragon no longer than her hand.

They set off down the dusky street together, and
Ged remarked as they went along, "In Gont they
say Gontish women are brave, but I never saw a
maiden there wear a dragon for a bracelet."

This made Yarrow laugh, and she answered him
straight, "This is only a harrekki, have you no harrekki on Gont?" Then she got shy for a moment
and hid her eyes.

"No, nor no dragons. Is not the creature a
dragon?"

"A little one, that lives in oak trees, and eats wasps and worms and sparrows' eggs — it grows no greater than this. Oh, Sir, my brother has told me often of the pet you had, the wild thing, the otak — do you have it still?"

"No. No longer."

Vetch turned to him as if with a question, but he held his tongue and asked nothing till much later, when the two of them sat alone over the stone firepit of Vetch's house.

Though he was the chief wizard in the whole island of Iffish, Vetch made his home in Ismay, this small town where he had been born, living with his youngest brother and sister. His father had been a sea-trader of some means, and the house was spacious and strong-beamed, with much homely wealth of pottery and fine weaving and vessels of bronze and brass on carven shelves and chests. A great Taonian harp stood in one corner of the main room, and Yarrow's tapestry-loom in another, its tall frame inlaid with ivory. There Vetch for all his plain quiet ways was both a powerful wizard and a lord in his own house. There were a couple of old servants, prospering along with the house, and the brother, a cheerful lad, and Yarrow, quick and silent as a little fish, who served the two friends their supper and ate with them, listening to their talk, and afterwards slipped off to her own room.

All things here were well-founded, peaceful, and assured; and Ged looking about him at the firelit room said, "This is how a man should live," and sighed.

"Well, it's one good way," said Vetch. "There are others. Now, lad, tell me if you can what things have come to you and gone from you since we last spoke, two years ago. And tell me what journey you are on, since I see well that you won't stay long with us this time."

Ged told him, and when he was done Vetch sat pondering for a long while. Then he said, "I'll go with you, Ged."

"No."

"I think I will."

"No, Estarriol. This is no task or bane of yours. I began this evil course alone, I will finish it alone, I do not want any other to suffer from it — you least of all, you who tried to keep my hand from the evil act in the very beginning, Estarriol —"

"Pride was ever your mind's master," his friend said smiling, as if they talked of a matter of small concern to either. "Now think: it is your quest, assuredly, but if the quest fails, should there not be another there who might bear warning to the Archipelago? For the shadow would be a fearful power then. And if you defeat the thing, should there not be another there who will tell of it in the

Archipelago, that the Deed may be known and sung? I know I can be of no use to you; yet I think I should go with you."

So entreated Ged could not deny his friend, but he said, "I should not have stayed this day here. I knew it, but I stayed."

"Wizards do not meet by chance, lad," said Vetch. "And after all, as you said yourself, I was with you at the beginning of your journey. It is right that I should follow you to its end." He put new wood on the fire, and they sat gazing into the flames a while.

"There is one I have not heard of since that night on Roke Knoll, and I had no heart to ask any at the School of him: Jasper, I mean."

"He never won his staff. He left Roke that same summer, and went to the Island of O to be sorcerer in the Lord's household at O-tokne. I know no more of him than that."

Again they were silent, watching the fire and enjoying (since it was a bitter night) the warmth on their legs and faces as they sat on the broad coping of the firepit, their feet almost among the coals.

Ged said at last, speaking low, "There is a thing that I fear, Estarriol. I fear it more if you are with me when I go. There in the Hands in the dead end of the inlet I turned upon the shadow, it was within my hands' reach, and I seized it—I tried to seize it. And there was nothing I could hold. I could not defeat it. It fled, I followed. But that may happen again, and yet again. I have no power over the thing. There may be neither death nor triumph to end this quest; nothing to sing of; no end. It may be I must spend my life running from sea to sea and land to land on an endless vain venture, a shadow-quest."

"Avert!" said Vetch, turning his left hand in the gesture that turns aside the ill chance spoken of. For all his somber thoughts this made Ged grin a little, for it is rather a child's charm than a wizard's; there was always such village innocence in Vetch. Yet also he was keen, shrewd, direct to the center of a thing. He said now, "That is a grim thought and I trust a false one. I guess rather that what I saw begin, I may see end. Somehow you will learn its nature, its being, what it is, and so hold and bind and vanquish it. Though that is a hard question: what is it . . . There is a thing that worries me, I do not understand it. It seems the shadow now goes in your shape, or a kind of likeness of you at least, as they saw it on Vemish and as I saw it here in Iffish. How may that be, and why, and why did it never do so in the Archipelago?"

"They say, *Rules change in the Reaches*."

"Aye, a true saying, I can tell you. There are good spells I learned on Roke that have no power here, or go all awry; and also there are spells worked here I never learned on Roke. Every land has its own powers, and the farther one goes from the Inner Lands, the less one can guess about those powers and their governance. But I do not think it is only that which works this change in the shadow."

"Nor do I. I think that, when I ceased to flee from it and turned against it, that turning of my will upon it gave it shape and form, even though the same act prevented it from taking my strength from me. All my acts have their echo in it; it is my creature."

"In Osskil it named you, and so stopped any wizardry you might have used against it. Why did it not do so again, there in the Hands?"

"I do not know. Perhaps it is only from my weakness that it draws the strength to speak. Almost with my own tongue it speaks: for how did it know my name? How did it know my name? I have racked my brains on that over all the seas since I left Gont, and I cannot see the answer. Maybe it cannot speak at all in its own form or formlessness, but only with borrowed tongue, as a gebbeth. I do not know."

"Then you must beware meeting it in gebbeth-form a second time."

"I think," Ged replied, stretching out his hands to the red coals as if he felt an inward chill, "I think

I will not. It is bound to me now as I am to it. It cannot get so far free of me as to seize any other man and empty him of will and being, as it did Skiorh. It can possess me. If ever I weaken again, and try to escape from it, to break the bond, it will possess me. And yet, when I held it with all the strength I had, it became mere vapor, and escaped from me . . . And so it will again, and yet it cannot really escape, for I can always find it. I am bound to the foul cruel thing, and will be forever, unless I can learn the word that masters it: its name."

Brooding his friend asked, "Are there names in the dark realms?"

"Gensher the Archmage said there are not. My master Ogion said otherwise."

*"Infinite are the arguments of mages,"* Vetch quoted, with a smile that was somewhat grim.

"She who served the Old Power on Osskil swore that the Stone would tell me the shadow's name, but that I count for little. However there was also a dragon, who offered to trade that name for his own, to be rid of me; and I have thought that, where mages argue, dragons may be wise."

"Wise, but unkind. But what dragon is this? You did not tell me you had been talking with dragons since I saw you last."

They talked together late that night, and though always they came back to the bitter matter of what lay before Ged, yet their pleasure in being together overrode all; for the love between them was strong and steadfast, unshaken by time or chance. In the morning Ged woke beneath his friend's roof, and while he was still drowsy he felt such wellbeing as if he were in some place wholly defended from evil and harm. All day long a little of this dream-peace clung to his thoughts, and he took it, not as a good omen, but as a gift. It seemed likely to him that leaving this house he would leave the last haven he was to know, and so while the short dream lasted he would be happy in it.

Having affairs he must see to before he left Iffish, Vetch went off to other villages of the island with the lad who served him as prentice-sorcerer. Ged stayed with Yarrow and her brother, called Murre, who was between her and Vetch in age. He seemed not much more than a boy, for there was no gift or scourge of mage-power in him, and he had never been anywhere but Iffish, Tok, and Holp, and his life was easy and untroubled. Ged watched him with wonder and some envy, and exactly so he watched Ged: to each it seemed very queer that the other, so different, yet was his own age, nineteen years. Ged marveled how one who had lived nineteen years could be so carefree. Admiring Murre's comely, cheerful face he felt himself to be all lank and harsh, never guessing that Murre envied him even the scars that scored his face, and thought them the track of a dragon's claws and the very rune and sign of a hero.

The two young men were thus somewhat shy with each other, but as for Yarrow she soon lost her awe of Ged, being in her own house and mistress of it. He was very gentle with her, and many were the questions she asked of him, for Vetch, she said, would never tell her anything. She kept busy those two days making dry wheatcakes for the voyagers to carry, and wrapping up dried fish and meat and other such provender to stock their boat, until Ged told her to stop, for he did not plan to sail clear to Selidor without a halt.

"Where is Selidor?"

"Very far out in the Western Reach, where dragons are as common as mice."

"Best stay in the East then, our dragons are as small as mice. There's your meat, then; you're sure that's enough? Listen, I don't understand: you and my brother both are mighty wizards, you wave your hand and mutter and the thing is done. Why do you get hungry, then? When it comes supper-time at sea, why not say, *Meat-pie!* and the meat-pie appears, and you eat it?"

"Well, we could do so. But we don't much wish to eat our words, as they say. *Meat-pie!* is only a word, after all . . . We can make it odorous, and savorous, and even filling, but it remains a word. It fools the stomach and gives no strength to the hungry man."

"Wizards, then, are not cooks," said Murre, who was sitting across the kitchen hearth from Ged, carving a box-lid of fine wood; he was a woodworker by trade, though not a very zealous one.

"Nor are cooks wizards, alas," said Yarrow on her knees to see if the last batch of cakes baking on the hearth-bricks was getting brown. "But I still don't understand, Sparrowhawk. I have seen my brother, and even his prentice, make light in a dark place only by saying one word: and the light shines, it is bright, not a word but a light you can see your way by!"

"Aye," Ged answered. "Light is a power. A great power, by which we exist, but which exists beyond our needs, in itself. Sunlight and starlight are time, and time is light. In the sunlight, in the days and years, life is. In a dark place life may call upon the light, naming it. But usually when you see a wizard name or call upon some thing, some object to appear, that is not the same, he calls upon no power greater than himself, and what appears is an illusion only. To summon a thing that is not there at all, to call it by speaking its true name, that is a great mastery, not lightly used. Not for mere hunger's sake. Yarrow, your little dragon has stolen a cake."

Yarrow had listened so hard, gazing at Ged as he spoke, that she had not seen the harrekki scuttle down from its warm perch on the kettle-hook over the hearth and seize a wheatcake bigger than itself. She took the small scaly creature on her knee and fed it bits and crumbs, while she pondered what Ged had told her.

"So then you would not summon up a real meat-pie lest you disturb what my brother is always talking about—I forget its name—"

"Equilibrium," Ged replied soberly, for she was very serious.

"Yes. But, when you were shipwrecked, you sailed from the place in a boat woven mostly of spells, and it didn't leak water. Was it illusion?"

"Well, partly it was illusion, because I am uneasy seeing the sea through great holes in my boat, so I patched them for the looks of the thing. But the strength of the boat was not illusion, nor summoning, but made with another kind of art, a binding-spell. The wood was bound as one whole, one entire thing, a boat. What is a boat but a thing that doesn't leak water?"

"I've bailed some that do," said Murre.

"Well, mine leaked, too, unless I was constantly

seeing to the spell." He bent down from his corner seat and took a cake from the bricks, and juggled it in his hands. "I too have stolen a cake."

"You have burned fingers, then. And when you're starving on the waste water between the far isles you'll think of that cake and say, *Ah! had I not stolen that cake I might eat it now, alas!*—I shall eat my brother's, so he can starve with you—"

"Thus is Equilibrium maintained," Ged remarked, while she took and munched a hot, half-toasted cake; and this made her giggle and choke. But presently looking serious again she said, "I wish I could truly understand what you tell me. I am too stupid."

"Little sister," Ged said, "it is I that have no skill explaining. If we had more time—"

"We will have more time," Yarrow said. "When my brother comes back home, you will come with him, for a while at least, won't you?"

"If I can," he answered gently.

There was a little pause; and Yarrow asked, watching the harrekki climb back to its perch, "Tell me just this, if it is not a secret: what other great powers are there besides the light?"

"It is no secret. All power is one in source and end, I think. Years and distances, stars and candles, water and wind and wizardry, the craft in a man's hand and the wisdom in a tree's root: they all arise together. My name, and yours, and the true name of the sun, or a spring of water, or an unborn child, all are syllables of the great word that is very slowly spoken by the shining of the stars. There is no other power. No other name."

Staying his knife on the carved wood, Murre asked, "What of death?"

The girl listened, her shining black head bent down.

"For a word to be spoken," Ged answered slowly, "there must be silence. Before, and after." Then all at once he got up, saying, "I have no right to speak of these things. The word that was mine to say I said wrong. It is better that I keep still; I will not speak again. Maybe there is no true power but the dark." And he left the fireside and the warm kitchen, taking up his cloak and going out alone into the drizzling cold rain of winter in the streets.

"He is under a curse," Murre said, gazing somewhat fearfully after him.

"I think this voyage he is on leads him to his death," the girl said, "and he fears that, yet he goes on." She lifted her head as if she watched, through the red flame of the fire, the course of a boat that came through the seas of winter alone, and went on out into empty seas. Then her eyes filled with tears a moment, but she said nothing.

Vetch came home the next day, and took his

leave of the notables of Ismay, who were most un-willing to let him go off to sea in midwinter on a mortal quest not even his own; but though they might reproach him, there was nothing at all they could do to stop him. Growing weary of old men who nagged him, he said, "I am yours, by parent-age and custom and by duty undertaken towards you. I am your wizard. But it is time you recalled that, though I am a servant, I am not your servant. When I am free to come back I will come back: till then, farewell."

At daybreak, as grey light welled up in the east from the sea, the two young men set forth in *Lookfar* from the harbor of Ismay, raising a brown, strong-woven sail to the north wind. On the dock Yarrow stood and watched them go, as sailors' wives and sisters stand on all the shores of all Earthsea watch-ing their men go out on the sea, and they do not wave or call aloud, but stand still in hooded cloak of grey or brown, there on the shore that dwindles smaller and smaller from the boat while the water grows wide between.

# CHAPTER 10

# THE OPEN SEA

**THE HAVEN NOW WAS SUNK** from sight and *Look-far*'s painted eyes, wave-drenched, looked ahead on seas ever wider and more desolate. In two days and nights the companions made the crossing from Iffish to Soders Island, a hundred miles of foul weather and contrary winds. They stayed in port there only briefly, long enough to refill a waterskin, and to buy a tar-smeared sailcloth to protect some of their gear in the undecked boat from seawater and rain. They had not provided this earlier, because ordinarily a wizard looks after such small conveniences by way of spells, the very least and commonest kind of spells, and indeed it takes little more magic to freshen seawater and so save the bother of carrying fresh water. But Ged seemed most unwilling to use his craft, or to let Vetch use his. He said only, "It's better not," and his friend did not ask or argue. For as the wind first filled their sail, both had felt a heavy foreboding, cold as that winter wind. Haven, harbor, peace, safety, all that was behind. They had turned away. They went now a way in which all events were perilous, and no acts were meaningless. On the course on which they were embarked, the saying of the least spell might change chance and move the balance of power and of doom: for they went now toward the very center of that balance, toward the place where light and darkness meet. Those who travel thus say no word carelessly.

Sailing out again and coasting round the shores of Soders, where white snowfields faded up into foggy hills, Ged took the boat southward again, and now they entered waters where the great traders of the Archipelago never come, the outmost fringes of the Reach.

Vetch asked no question about their course, knowing that Ged did not choose it but went as he must go. As Soders Island grew small and pale behind them, and the waves hissed and smacked under the prow, and the great grey plain of water circled them all round clear to the edge of the sky, Ged asked, "What lands lie ahead this course?"

"Due south of Soders there are no lands at all. Southeast you go a long way and find little: Pelimer, Kornay, Gosk, and Astowell which is also called Lastland. Beyond it, the Open Sea."

"What to the southwest?"

"Rolameny, which is one of our East Reach isles,

and some small islets round about it; then nothing till you enter the South Reach: Rood, and Toom, and the Isle of the Ear where men do not go."

"We may," Ged said wryly.

"I'd rather not," said Vetch. "That is a disagreeable part of the world, they say, full of bones and portents. Sailors say that there are stars to be seen from the waters by the Isle of the Ear and Far Sorr that cannot be seen anywhere else, and that have never been named."

"Aye, there was a sailor on the ship that brought me first to Roke who spoke of that. And he told tales of the Raft-Folk in the far South Reach, who never come to land but once a year, to cut the great logs for their rafts, and the rest of the year, all the days and months, they drift on the currents of ocean, out of sight of any land. I'd like to see those raft-villages."

"I would not," said Vetch grinning. "Give me land, and land-folk; the sea in its bed and I in mine . . ."

"I wish I could have seen all the cities of the Archipelago," Ged said as he held the sail-rope, watching the wide grey wastes before them. "Havnor at the world's heart, and Éa where the myths were born, and Shelieth of the Fountains on Way; all the cities and the great lands. And the small lands, the strange lands of the Outer Reaches, them too. To sail right down the Dragons' Run, away in the west. Or to sail north into the ice-floes, clear to Hogen Land. Some say that is a land greater than all the Archipelago, and others say it is mere reefs and rocks with ice between. No one knows. I should like to see the whales in the northern seas . . . But I cannot. I must go where I am bound to go, and turn my back on the bright shores. I was in too much haste, and now have no time left. I traded all the sunlight and the cities and the distant lands for a handful of power, for a shadow, for the dark." So, as the mage-born will, Ged made his fear and regret into a song, a brief lament, half-sung, that was not for himself alone; and his friend replying spoke the hero's words from the *Deed of Erreth-Akbe,* "O may I see the earth's bright hearth once more, the white towers of Havnor . . ."

So they sailed on their narrow course over the wide forsaken waters. The most they saw that day was a school of silver pannies swimming south, but never a dolphin leapt nor did the flight of gull or murre or tern break the grey air. As the east darkened and the west grew red, Vetch brought out food and divided it between them and said, "Here's the last of the ale. I drink to the one who thought to put the keg aboard for thirsty men in cold weather: my sister Yarrow."

At that Ged left off his bleak thoughts and his

gazing ahead over the sea, and he saluted Yarrow more earnestly, perhaps, than Vetch. The thought of her brought to his mind the sense of her wise and childish sweetness. She was not like any person he had known. (What young girl had he ever known at all? but he never thought of that.) "She is like a little fish, a minnow, that swims in a clear creek," he said, " — defenseless, yet you cannot catch her."

At this Vetch looked straight at him, smiling. "You are a mage born," he said. "Her true name is Kest." In the Old Speech, *kest* is minnow, as Ged well knew; and this pleased him to the heart. But after a while he said in a low voice, "You should not have told me her name, maybe."

But Vetch, who had not done so lightly, said, "Her name is safe with you as mine is. And, besides, you knew it without my telling you . . ."

Red sank to ashes in the west, and ash-grey sank to black. All the sea and sky were wholly dark. Ged stretched out in the bottom of the boat to sleep, wrapped in his cloak of wool and fur. Vetch, holding the sail-rope, sang softly from the *Deed of Enlad,* where the song tells how the mage Morred the White left Havnor in his oarless longship, and coming to the island Soléa saw Elfarran in the orchards in the spring. Ged slept before the song came to the sorry end of their love, Morred's death, the ruin of Enlad, the sea-waves, vast and bitter, whelming the orchards of Soléa. Towards midnight he woke, and watched again while Vetch slept. The little boat ran sharp over choppy seas, fleeing the strong wind that leaned on her sail, running blind through the night. But the overcast had broken, and before dawn the thin moon shining between brown-edged clouds shed a weak light on the sea.

"The moon wanes to her dark," Vetch murmured, awake in the dawn, when for a while the cold wind dropped. Ged looked up at the white half-ring above the paling eastern waters, but said nothing. The dark of the moon that follows first after Sunreturn is called the Fallows, and is the contrary pole of the days of the Moon and the Long Dance in summer. It is an unlucky time for travelers and for the sick; children are not given their true name during the Fallows, and no Deeds are sung, nor swords nor edge-tools sharpened, nor oaths sworn. It is the dark axis of the year, when things done are ill done.

Three days out from Soders they came, following sea-birds and shore-wrack, to Pelimer, a small isle humped high above the high grey seas. Its people spoke Hardic, but in their own fashion, strange even to Vetch's ears. The young men came ashore there for fresh water and a respite from the sea, and at first were well received, with wonder and commotion. There was a sorcerer in the main town of

the island, but he was mad. He would talk only of
the great serpent that was eating at the foundations
of Pelimer so that soon the island must go adrift
like a boat cut from her moorings, and slide out
over the edge of the world. At first he greeted the
young wizards courteously, but as he talked about
the serpent he began to look askance at Ged: and
then he fell to railing at them there in the street,
calling them spies and servants of the Sea-Snake.
The Pelimerians looked dourly at them after that,
since though mad he was their sorcerer. So Ged
and Vetch made no long stay, but set forth again
before nightfall, going always south and east.

In these days and nights of sailing Ged never
spoke of the shadow, nor directly of his quest;
and the nearest Vetch came to asking any question was (as they followed the same course farther
and farther out and away from the known lands
of Earthsea)—"Are you sure?—" To this Ged
answered only, "Is the iron sure where the magnet lies?" Vetch nodded and they went on, no more
being said by either. But from time to time they
talked of the crafts and devices that mages of old
days had used to find out the hidden name of baneful powers and beings: how Nereger of Paln had
learned the Black Mage's name from overhearing
the conversation of dragons, and how Morred had
seen his enemy's name written by falling rain-

drops in the dust of the battlefield of the Plains of
Enlad. They spoke of finding-spells, and invocations, and those Answerable Questions which only
the Master Patterner of Roke can ask. But often
Ged would end by murmuring words which Ogion
had said to him on the shoulder of Gont Mountain in an autumn long ago: "To hear, one must
be silent . . ." And he would fall silent, and ponder,
hour by hour, always watching the sea ahead of
the boat's way. Sometimes it seemed to Vetch that
his friend saw, across the waves and miles and grey
days yet to come, the thing they followed and the
dark end of their voyage.

They passed between Kornay and Gosk in foul
weather, seeing neither isle in the fog and rain, and
knowing they had passed them only on the next
day when they saw ahead of them an isle of pin-
nacled cliffs above which sea-gulls wheeled in huge
flocks whose mewing clamor could be heard from
far over the sea. Vetch said, "That will be Astowell,
from the look of it. Lastland. East and south of it
the charts are empty."

"Yet they who live there may know of farther
lands," Ged answered.

"Why do you say so?" Vetch asked, for Ged had
spoken uneasily; and his answer to this again was
halting and strange. "Not there," he said, gazing at
Astowell ahead, and past it, or through it— "Not

there. Not on the sea. Not on the sea but on dry land: what land? Before the springs of the open sea, beyond the sources, behind the gates of daylight—"

Then he fell silent, and when he spoke again it was in an ordinary voice, as if he had been freed from a spell or a vision, and had no clear memory of it.

The port of Astowell, a creek-mouth between rocky heights, was on the northern shore of the isle, and all the huts of the town faced north and west; it was as if the island turned its face, though from so far away, always towards Earthsea, towards mankind.

Excitement and dismay attended the arrival of strangers, in a season when no boat had ever braved the seas round Astowell. The women all stayed in the wattle huts, peering out the door, hiding their children behind their skirts, drawing back fearfully into the darkness of the huts as the strangers came up from the beach. The men, lean fellows ill-clothed against the cold, gathered in a solemn circle about Vetch and Ged, and each one held a stone hand-axe or a knife of shell. But once their fear was past they made the strangers very welcome, and there was no end to their questions. Seldom did any ship come to them even from Soders or Rolameny, they having nothing to trade for bronze or fine wares; they had not even any wood. Their boats were coracles woven of reed, and it was a brave sailor who would go as far as Gosk or Kornay in such a craft. They dwelt all alone here at the edge of all the maps. They had no witch or sorcerer, and seemed not to recognize the young wizards' staffs for what they were, admiring them only for the precious stuff they were made of, wood. Their chief or Isle-Man was very old, and he alone of his people had ever before seen a man born in the Archipelago. Ged, therefore, was a marvel to them; the men brought their little sons to look at the Archipelagan, so they might remember him when they were old. They had never heard of Gont, only of Havnor and Éa, and took him for a Lord of Havnor. He did his best to answer their questions about the white city he had never seen. But he was restless as the evening wore on, and at last he asked the men of the village, as they sat crowded round the firepit in the lodgehouse in the reeking warmth of the goatdung and broom-faggots that were all their fuel, "What lies eastward of your land?"

They were silent, some grinning others grim.

The old Isle-Man answered, "The sea."

"There is no land beyond?"

"This is Lastland. There is no land beyond. There is nothing but water till world's edge."

"These are wise men, father," said a younger man, "seafarers, voyagers. Maybe they know of a land we do not know of."

"There is no land east of this land," said the old man, and he looked long at Ged, and spoke no more to him.

The companions slept that night in the smoky warmth of the lodge. Before daylight Ged roused his friend, whispering, "Estarriol, wake. We cannot stay, we must go."

"Why so soon?" Vetch asked, full of sleep.

"Not soon—late. I have followed too slow. It has found the way to escape me, and so doom me. It must not escape me, for I must follow it however far it goes. If I lose it I am lost."

"Where do we follow it?"

"Eastward. Come. I filled the waterskins."

So they left the lodge before any in the village was awake, except a baby that cried a little in the darkness of some hut, and fell still again. By the vague starlight they found the way down to the creek-mouth, and untied *Lookfar* from the rock cairn where she had been made fast, and pushed her out into the black water. So they set out eastward from Astowell into the Open Sea, on the first day of the Fallows, before sunrise.

That day they had clear skies. The world's wind

was cold and gusty from the northeast, but Ged
had raised the magewind: the first act of magery he
had done since he left the Isle of the Hands. They
sailed very fast due eastward. The boat shuddered
with the great, smoking, sunlit waves that hit her
as she ran, but she went gallantly as her builder had
promised, answering the magewind as true as any
spell-enwoven ship of Roke.

Ged spoke not at all that morning, except to
renew the power of the wind-spell or to keep a
charmed strength in the sail, and Vetch finished
his sleep, though uneasily, in the stern of the boat.
At noon they ate. Ged doled their food out spar-
ingly, and the portent of this was plain, but both of
them chewed their bit of salt fish and wheaten cake,
and neither said anything.

All afternoon they cleaved eastward never turning nor slackening pace. Once Ged broke his silence, saying, "Do you hold with those who think
the world is all landless sea beyond the Outer
Reaches, or with those who imagine other Archi-
pelagoes or vast undiscovered lands on the other
face of the world?"

"At this time," said Vetch, "I hold with those
who think the world has but one face, and he who
sails too far will fall off the edge of it."

Ged did not smile; there was no mirth left in

him. "Who knows what a man might meet, out there? Not we, who keep always to our coasts and shores."

"Some have sought to know, and have not returned. And no ship has ever come to us from lands we do not know."

Ged made no reply.

All that day, all that night they went driven by the powerful wind of magery over the great swells of ocean, eastward. Ged kept watch from dusk till dawn, for in darkness the force that drew or drove him grew stronger yet. Always he watched ahead, though his eyes in the moonless night could see no more than the painted eyes aside the boat's blind prow. By daybreak his dark face was grey with weariness, and he was so cramped with cold that he could hardly stretch out to rest. He said whispering, "Hold the magewind from the west, Estarriol," and then he slept.

There was no sunrise, and presently rain came beating across the bow from the northeast. It was no storm, only the long, cold winds and rains of winter. Soon all things in the open boat were wet through, despite the sailcloth cover they had bought; and Vetch felt as if he too were soaked clear to the bone; and Ged shivered in his sleep. In pity for his friend, and perhaps for himself, Vetch tried to turn aside for a little that rude ceaseless wind that bore the rain. But though, following Ged's will, he could keep the magewind strong and steady, his weatherworking had small power here so far from land, and the wind of the Open Sea did not listen to his voice.

And at this a certain fear came into Vetch, as he began to wonder how much wizardly power would be left to him and Ged, if they went on and on away from the lands where men were meant to live.

Ged watched again that night, and all night held the boat eastward. When day came the world's wind slackened somewhat, and the sun shone fitfully; but the great swells ran so high that *Lookfar* must tilt and climb up them as if they were hills, and hang at the hillcrest and plunge suddenly, and climb up the next again, and the next, and the next, unending.

In the evening of that day Vetch spoke out of long silence. "My friend," he said, "you spoke once as if sure we would come to land at last. I would not question your vision but for this, that it might be a trick, a deception made by that which you follow, to lure you on farther than a man can go over ocean. For our power may change and weaken on strange seas. And a shadow does not tire, or starve, or drown."

They sat side by side on the thwart, yet Ged looked at him now as if from a distance, across a wide abyss. His eyes were troubled, and he was slow to answer.

At last he said, "Estarriol, we are coming near."

Hearing his words, his friend knew them to be true. He was afraid, then. But he put his hand on Ged's shoulder and said only, "Well, then, good; that is good."

Again that night Ged watched, for he could not sleep in the dark. Nor would he sleep when the third day came. Still they ran with that ceaseless, light, terrible swiftness over the sea, and Vetch wondered at Ged's power that could hold so strong a magewind hour after hour, here on the Open Sea where Vetch felt his own power all weakened and astray. And they went on, until it seemed to Vetch that what Ged had spoken would come true, and they were going beyond the sources of the sea and eastward behind the gates of daylight. Ged stayed forward in the boat, looking ahead as always. But he was not watching the ocean now, or not the ocean that Vetch saw, a waste of heaving water to the rim of the sky. In Ged's eyes there was a dark vision that overlapped and veiled the grey sea and the grey sky, and the darkness grew, and the veil thickened. None of this was visible to Vetch, except when he looked at his friend's face; then he too saw the darkness for a moment. They went on, and on. And it was as if, though one wind drove them in one boat, Vetch went east over the world's sea, while Ged went alone into a realm where there was no east or west, no rising or setting of the sun, or of the stars.

Ged stood up suddenly in the prow, and spoke aloud. The magewind dropped. *Lookfar* lost headway, and rose and fell on the vast surges like a chip of wood. Though the world's wind blew strong as ever straight from the north now, the brown sail hung slack, unstirred. And so the boat hung on the waves, swung by their great slow swinging, but going no direction.

Ged said, "Take down the sail," and Vetch did so quickly, while Ged unlashed the oars and set them in the locks and bent his back to rowing.

Vetch, seeing only the waves heaving up and down clear to the end of sight, could not understand why they went now by oars; but he waited, and presently he was aware that the world's wind was growing faint and the swells diminishing. The climb and plunge of the boat grew less and less, till at last she seemed to go forward under Ged's strong oarstrokes over water that lay almost still, as in a land-locked bay. And though Vetch could not see what Ged saw, when between his strokes he looked ever and again over his shoulder at what lay before the boat's way—though Vetch could not see the dark slopes beneath unmoving stars, yet he began to see with his wizard's eye a darkness that welled up in the hollows of the waves all around the boat, and he saw the billows grow low and sluggish as they were choked with sand.

If this were an enchantment of illusion, it was powerful beyond belief; to make the Open Sea seem land. Trying to collect his wits and courage, Vetch spoke the Revelation-spell, watching between each slow-syllabled word for change or tremor of illusion in this strange drying and shallowing of the abyss of ocean. But there was none. Perhaps the spell, though it should affect only his own vision and not the magic at work about them, had no power here. Or perhaps there was no illusion, and they had come to world's end.

Unheeding, Ged rowed always slower, looking over his shoulder, choosing a way among channels or shoals and shallows that he alone could see. The boat shuddered as her keel dragged. Under that keel lay the vast deeps of the sea, yet they were aground. Ged drew the oars up rattling in their locks, and that noise was terrible, for there was no other sound. All sounds of water, wind, wood, sail, were gone, lost in a huge profound silence that might have been unbroken forever. The boat lay motionless. No breath of wind moved. The sea had turned to sand, shadowy, unstirred. Nothing moved in the dark sky or on that dry unreal ground that went on and on into gathering darkness all around the boat as far as eye could see.

Ged stood up, and took his staff, and lightly stepped over the side of the boat. Vetch thought to see him fall and sink down in the sea, the sea that surely was there behind this dry, dim veil that hid away water, sky, and light. But there was no sea anymore. Ged walked away from the boat. The dark sand showed his footprints where he went, and whispered a little under his step.

His staff began to shine, not with the werelight but with a clear white glow, that soon grew so bright that it reddened his fingers where they held the radiant wood.

He strode forward, away from the boat, but in no direction. There were no directions here, no north or south or east or west, only towards and away.

To Vetch, watching, the light he bore seemed like a great slow star that moved through the darkness. And the darkness about it thickened, blackened, drew together. This also Ged saw, watching always ahead through the light. And after a while he saw at the faint outermost edge of the light a shadow that came towards him over the sand.

At first it was shapeless, but as it drew nearer it took on the look of a man. An old man it seemed, grey and grim, coming towards Ged; but even as

Ged saw his father the smith in that figure, he saw
that it was not an old man but a young one. It was
Jasper: Jasper's insolent handsome young face, and
silver-clasped grey cloak, and stiff stride. Hateful
was the look he fixed on Ged across the dark inter-
vening air. Ged did not stop, but slowed his pace,
and as he went forward he raised his staff up a little
higher. It brightened, and in its light the look of
Jasper fell from the figure that approached, and
it became Pechvarry. But Pechvarry's face was all
bloated and pallid like the face of a drowned man,
and he reached out his hand strangely as if beck-
oning. Still Ged did not stop, but went forward,
though there were only a few yards left between
them now. Then the thing that faced him changed
utterly, spreading out to either side as if it opened
enormous thin wings, and it writhed, and swelled,
and shrank again. Ged saw in it for an instant Skiorh's white face, and then a pair of clouded, staring
eyes, and then suddenly a fearful face he did not
know, man or monster, with writhing lips and eyes
that were like pits going back into black emptiness.

At that Ged lifted up the staff high, and the radiance of it brightened intolerably, burning with so
white and great a light that it compelled and har-
rowed even that ancient darkness. In that light all
form of man sloughed off the thing that came to-

wards Ged. It drew together and shrank and black-ened, crawling on four short taloned legs upon the sand. But still it came forward, lifting up to him a blind unformed snout without lips or ears or eyes. As they came right together it became utterly black in the white mage-radiance that burned about it, and it heaved itself upright. In silence, man and shadow met face to face, and stopped.

Aloud and clearly, breaking that old silence, Ged spoke the shadow's name and in the same mo-ment the shadow spoke without lips or tongue, say-ing the same word: "Ged." And the two voices were one voice.

Ged reached out his hands, dropping his staff, and took hold of his shadow, of the black self that reached out to him. Light and darkness met, and joined, and were one.

But to Vetch, watching in terror through the dark twilight from far off over the sand, it seemed that Ged was overcome, for he saw the clear ra-diance fail and grow dim. Rage and despair filled him, and he sprang out on the sand to help his friend or die with him, and ran towards that small fading glimmer of light in the empty dusk of the dry land. But as he ran the sand sank under his feet, and he struggled in it as in quicksand, as through a heavy flow of water: until with a roar of noise and a glory of daylight, and the bitter cold of winter, and the bitter taste of salt, the world was restored to him and he floundered in the sudden, true, and living sea.

Nearby the boat rocked on the grey waves, empty. Vetch could see nothing else on the water; the battering wave-tops filled his eyes and blinded him. No strong swimmer, he struggled as best he could to the boat, and pulled himself up into her. Coughing and trying to wipe away the water that streamed from his hair, he looked about desperately, not knowing now which way to look. And at last he made out something dark among the waves, a long way off across what had been sand and now was wild water. Then he leapt to the oars and rowed mightily to his friend, and catching Ged's arms helped and hauled him up over the side.

Ged was dazed and his eyes stared as if they saw nothing, but there was no hurt to be seen on him. His staff, black yew-wood, all radiance quenched, was grasped in his right hand, and he would not let go of it. He said no word. Spent and soaked and shaking he lay huddled up against the mast, never looking at Vetch who raised the sail and turned the boat to catch the northeast wind. He saw nothing of the world until, straight ahead of their course, in the sky that darkened where the sun had set, between long clouds in a bay of clear blue light, the new moon shone: a ring of ivory, a rim of horn, reflected sunlight shining across the ocean of the dark.

Ged lifted his face and gazed at that remote bright crescent in the west.

He gazed for a long time, and then he stood up erect, holding his staff in his two hands as a warrior holds his long sword. He looked about at the sky, the sea, the brown swelling sail above him, his friend's face.

"Estarriol," he said, "look, it is done. It is over." He laughed. "The wound is healed," he said, "I am whole, I am free." Then he bent over and hid his face in his arms, weeping like a boy.

Until that moment Vetch had watched him with an anxious dread, for he was not sure what had happened there in the dark land. He did not know if this was Ged in the boat with him, and his hand had been for hours ready to the anchor, to stave in the boat's planking and sink her there in midsea, rather than carry back to the harbors of Earthsea the evil thing that he feared might have taken Ged's look and form. Now when he saw his friend and heard him speak, his doubt vanished. And he began to see the truth, that Ged had neither lost nor won but, naming the shadow of his death

with his own name, had made himself whole: a
man: who, knowing his whole true self, cannot be
used or possessed by any power other than himself,
and whose life therefore is lived for life's sake and
never in the service of ruin, or pain, or hatred, or
the dark. In the *Creation of Éa,* which is the oldest
song, it is said, "Only in silence the word, only in
dark the light, only in dying life: bright the hawk's
flight on the empty sky." That song Vetch sang
aloud now as he held the boat westward, going before the cold wind of the winter night that blew at
their backs from the vastness of the Open Sea.

Eight days they sailed and eight again, before
they came in sight of land. Many times they had to
refill their waterskin with spell-sweetened water of
the sea; and they fished, but even when they called
out fisherman's charms they caught very little, for
the fish of the Open Sea do not know their own
names and pay no heed to magic. When they had
nothing left to eat but a few scraps of smoked meat
Ged remembered what Yarrow had said when he
stole the cake from the hearth, that he would regret his theft when he came to hunger on the sea;
but hungry as he was the remembrance pleased
him. For she had also said that he, with her brother,
would come home again.

The magewind had borne them for only three

days eastward, yet sixteen days they sailed westward to return. No men have ever returned from so far out on the Open Sea as did the young wizards Estarriol and Ged in the Fallows of winter in their open fishingboat. They met no great storms, and steered steadily enough by the compass and by the star Tolbegren, taking a course somewhat northward of their outbound way. Thus they did not come back to Astowell, but passing by Far Toly and Sneg without sighting them, first raised land off the southernmost cape of Koppish. Over the waves they saw cliffs of stone rise like a great fortress. Seabirds cried wheeling over the breakers, and smoke of the hearthfires of small villages drifted blue on the wind.

From there the voyage to Iffish was not long. They came in to Ismay harbor on a still, dark evening before snow. They tied up the boat *Lookfar* that had borne them to the coasts of death's kingdom and back, and went up through the narrow streets to the wizard's house. Their hearts were very light as they entered into the firelight and warmth under that roof; and Yarrow ran to meet them, crying with joy.

IF ESTARRIOL OF IFFISH KEPT his promise and made a song of that first great deed of Ged's, it has been lost. There is a tale told in the East Reach of a boat that ran aground, days out from any shore, over the abyss of ocean. In Iffish they say it was Estarriol who sailed that boat, but in Tok they say it was two fishermen blown by a storm far out on the Open Sea, and in Holp the tale is of a Holpish fisherman, and tells that he could not move his boat from the unseen sands it grounded on, and so wanders there yet. So of the song of the Shadow there remain only a few scraps of legend, carried like driftwood from isle to isle over the long years. But in the *Deed of Ged* nothing is told of that voyage nor of Ged's meeting with the shadow, before ever he sailed the Dragons' Run unscathed, or brought back the Ring of Erreth-Akbe from the Tombs of Atuan to Havnor, or came at last to Roke once more, as Archmage of all the islands of the world.

# AFTERWORD

ONCE UPON A TIME, a publisher asked me if I'd write a novel for teenagers. "Oh, no!" I said. "No, thanks very much, but I couldn't!"

It was the idea of writing with a specific audience in mind or a specific age of reader that scared me off. I'd published fantasy and science fiction, but I was interested in the form itself, not in who read it or how old they were. But maybe my real problem was that I'd spent so many years writing novels, sending them to publishers, and having them come back with a dull thud on the doormat that I had trouble comprehending that an actual publisher had really asked me to write a book . . .

He was Herman Schein of Parnassus Press in Berkeley, the publisher of my mother's books for children. He wanted to begin doing novels for older kids. When I said, "Oh, no!" he just said, "Well, think about it. Fantasy, maybe—whatever you like."

I thought about it. Slowly the idea sank in. Would writing for older kids be so different from just writing? Why? Despite what some adults seem to think, teenagers are fully human. And some of them read as intensely and keenly as if their life depended on it. Sometimes maybe it does.

And fantasy — pure, old-fashioned fantasy, not mixed with science fiction — I liked the idea. All my life I'd been reading about wizards, dragons, magic spells . . .

Back then, in 1967, wizards were all, more or less, Merlin and Gandalf. Old men, peaked hats, white beards. But this was to be a book for young people. Well, Merlin and Gandalf must have been young once, right? And when they were young, when they were fool kids, how did they learn to be wizards?

And there was my book.

Well, not instantly, of course. A novel takes a while to write. This one went pretty quickly and easily, though. I didn't have a plot outlined out when I started, but I knew what the story was. I knew who my Sparrowhawk was, and in a general way I knew where he was going — where he had to go, not only to learn to be a wizard, but to learn to be Ged. Then, as I wrote his story, what he did and said, where he went and the people he met, showed

me and told me what he had to do and where he
had to go next.

But *where* is as important in the realms of pure
imagination as it is here in mundanity. Before I
started to write the story, I got a big piece of poster-
board and drew the map. I drew all the islands of
Earthsea, the Archipelago, the Kargad Lands, the
Reaches. And I named them: Havnor, the great island at the middle of the world; Selidor, far out in
the west, and the Dragon's Run, and Hur-at-Hur,
and all the rest. But only as I sailed with Ged from
Gont did I begin to know the islands, one by one.
With him, I first came to Roke, and the Ninety
Isles, and Osskil, and farther east even than Astowell. And with him I first went to the dark, dry
country, the place across the wall where the dead
must go. A voyage long enough, strange enough,
great enough for one book.

Fantasy is now a branch of the publishing industry,
with many titles, many sequels, great expectations
of monster successes and movie tie-ins. In 1967
it was pretty much nowhere. Kid stuff. The only
adult fantasy novel most people had even heard
of was *The Lord of the Rings*. There were others,
some of them wonderful, but they mostly lurked

in small secondhand bookshops smelling of cats and mildew. I miss those bookshops now, the cats, the mildew, the thrill of discovery. Fantasy as an assembly-line commodity leaves me cold.

But I rejoice when I see it written as what it always was—literature—and recognized as such.

When *A Wizard of Earthsea* came out, there had not been a book like it. It was original—something new. Yet it was also conventional enough not to frighten reviewers. It was well received. The Boston Globe–Horn Book Award helped it. And the fact that fantasy isn't "for" a certain age but is a literature accessible to anybody who reads—that helped too. My wizard never got on the bestseller lists, but he kept on finding readers, year after year. The book has never been out of print.

The conventionality of the story, and its originality, reflect its existence within and partial subversion of an accepted, recognized tradition, one I grew up with. That is the tradition of fantastic tales and hero stories, which comes down to us like a great river from sources high in the mountains of Myth—a confluence of folk and fairy tale, classical epic, medieval and Renaissance and Eastern romance, romantic ballad, Victorian imaginative tale, and twentieth-century book of fantastic adventure such as T. H. White's Arthurian cycle and Tolkien's great book.

Most of this marvelous flood of literature was written for adults, but modernist literary ideology shunted it all to children. And kids could and did swim in it happily as in their native element, at least until some teacher or professor told them they had to come out, dry off, and breathe modernism ever after.

The part of the tradition that I knew best was mostly written (or rewritten for children) in England and northern Europe. The principal characters were men. If the story was heroic, the hero was a white man; most dark-skinned people were inferior or evil. If there was a woman in the story, she was a passive object of desire and rescue (a beautiful blond princess); active women (dark, witches) usually caused destruction or tragedy. Anyway, the stories weren't about the women. They were about men, what men did, and what was important to men.

It's in this sense that *A Wizard* was perfectly conventional. The hero does what a man is supposed to do: he uses his strength, wits, and courage to rise from humble beginnings to great fame and power, in a world where women are secondary, a man's world.

In other ways my story didn't follow the tradition. Its subversive elements attracted little attention, no doubt because I was deliberately sneaky

about them. A great many white readers in 1967
were not ready to accept a brown-skinned hero. But
they weren't expecting one. I didn't make an issue
of it, and you have to be well into the book before
you realize that Ged, like most of the characters,
isn't white.

His people, the Archipelagans, are various
shades of copper and brown, shading into black
in the South and East Reaches. The light-skinned
people among them have far-northern or Kargish
ancestors. The Kargish raiders in the first chapter
are white. Serret, who both as girl and woman be-
trays Ged, is white. Ged is copper-brown and his
friend Vetch is black. I was bucking the racist tradition, "making a statement" — but I made it quietly,
and it went almost unnoticed.

Alas, I had no power, at that time, to combat
the flat refusal of many cover departments to put
people of color on a book jacket. So, through many
later, lily-white Geds, Ruth Robbins's painting
for the first edition — the fine, strong profile of a
young man with copper-brown skin — was, to me,
the book's one true cover.

My story took off in its own direction, away
from the tradition, also in the whole matter of what
makes heroes and villains. Hero tales and adventure fantasies traditionally put the righteous hero
in a war against unrighteous enemies, which he

(usually) wins. This convention was and still is so dominant that it's taken for granted — "of course" a heroic fantasy is good guys fighting bad guys, the War of Good Against Evil.

But there are no wars in Earthsea. No soldiers, no armies, no battles. None of the militarism that came from the Arthurian saga and other sources and that by now, under the influence of fantasy war games, has become almost obligatory.

I didn't and don't think this way; my mind doesn't work in terms of war. My imagination refuses to limit all the elements that make an adventure story and make it exciting — danger, risk, challenge, courage — to battlefields. A hero whose heroism consists of killing people is uninteresting to me, and I detest the hormonal war orgies of our visual media, the mechanical slaughter of endless battalions of black-clad, yellow-toothed, red-eyed demons.

War as a moral metaphor is limited, limiting, and dangerous. By reducing the choices of action to "a war against" whatever-it-is, you divide the world into Me or Us (good) and Them or It (bad) and reduce the ethical complexity and moral richness of our life to Yes/No, On/Off. This is puerile, misleading, and degrading. In stories, it evades any solution but violence and offers the reader mere infantile reassurance. All too often the heroes of such fantasies behave exactly as the villains do, acting with mindless violence, but the hero is on the "right" side and therefore will win. Right makes might.

Or does might make right?

If war is the only game going, yes. Might makes right. Which is why I don't play war games.

To be the man he can be, Ged has to find out who and what his real enemy is. He has to find out what it means to be himself. That requires not a war but a search and a discovery. The search takes him through mortal danger, loss, and suffering. The discovery brings him victory, the kind of victory that isn't the end of a battle but the beginning of a life.

*Ursula K. Le Guin*

Turn the page for a sneak peek at
*The Tombs of Atuan*, the next adventure in
The EARTHSEA Cycle by Ursula K. Le Guin!

"COME HOME, TENAR! COME HOME!"

In the deep valley, in the twilight, the apple trees were on the eve of blossoming; here and there among the shadowed boughs one flower had opened early, rose and white, like a faint star. Down the orchard aisles, in the thick, new, wet grass, the little girl ran for the joy of running; hearing the call she did not come at once, but made a long circle before she turned her face toward home. The mother waiting in the doorway of the hut, with the firelight behind her, watched the tiny figure running and bobbing like a bit of thistledown blown over the darkening grass beneath the trees.

By the corner of the hut, scraping clean an earth-clotted hoe, the father said, "Why do you let your heart hang on the child? They're coming to take her away next month. For good. Might as well bury her and be done with it. What's the good of clinging to one you're bound to lose? She's no good to us. If they'd pay for her when they took her, which would be something, but they won't. They'll take her and that's an end of it."

The mother said nothing, watching the child who had stopped to look up through the trees. Over the high hills, above the orchards, the evening star shone piercing clear.

"She isn't ours, she never was since they came here and said she must be the Priestess at the Tombs. Why can't you see that?" The man's voice was harsh with complaint and bitterness. "You have four others. They'll stay here, and this one won't. So, don't set your heart on her. Let her go!"

"When the time comes," the woman said, "I will let her go." She bent to meet the child who came running on little, bare, white feet across the muddy ground, and gathered her up in her arms. As she turned to enter the hut she bent her head to kiss the child's hair, which was black; but her own hair, in the flicker of firelight from the hearth, was fair.

The man stood outside, his own feet bare and cold on the ground, the clear sky of spring darkening above him. His face in the dusk was full of grief, a dull, heavy, angry grief that he would never find the words to say. At last he shrugged, and followed his wife into the firelit room that rang with children's voices.

# CHAPTER I

# THE EATEN ONE

**ONE HIGH HORN SHRILLED AND** ceased. The silence that followed was shaken only by the sound of many footsteps keeping time with a drum struck softly at a slow heart-pace. Through cracks in the roof of the Hall of the Throne, gaps between columns where a whole section of masonry and tile had collapsed, unsteady sunlight shone aslant. It was an hour after sunrise. The air was still and cold. Dead leaves of weeds that had forced up between marble pavement-tiles were outlined with frost, and crackled, catching on the long black robes of the priestesses.

They came, four by four, down the vast hall between double rows of columns. The drum beat dully. No voice spoke, no eye watched. Torches carried by black-clad girls burned reddish in the shafts of sunlight, brighter in the dusk between. Outside, on the steps of the Hall of the Throne, the men stood, guards, trumpeters, drummers; within the great doors only women had come, dark-robed and hooded, walking slowly four by four toward the empty throne.

Two came, tall women looming in their black, one of them thin and rigid, the other heavy, swaying with the planting of her feet. Between these two walked a child of about six. She wore a straight white shift. Her head and arms and legs were bare, and she was barefoot. She looked extremely small. At the foot of the steps leading up to the throne, where the others now waited in dark rows, the two tall women halted. They pushed the child forward a little.

The throne on its high platform seemed to be curtained on each side with great webs of blackness dropping from the gloom of the roof; whether these were curtains, or only denser shadows, the eye could not make certain. The throne itself was black, with a dull glimmer of precious stones or gold on the arms and back, and it was huge. A man sitting in it would have been dwarfed; it was not of human dimensions. It was empty. Nothing sat in it but shadows.

Alone, the child climbed up four of the seven steps of red-veined marble. They were so broad and high that she had to get both feet onto one step before attempting the next. On the middle step, directly in front of the throne, stood a large, rough block of wood, hollowed out on top. The child knelt on both

knees and fitted her head into the hollow, turning it a
little sideways. She knelt there without moving.

A figure in a belted gown of white wool stepped
suddenly out of the shadows at the right of the
throne and strode down the steps to the child.
His face was masked with white. He held a sword
of polished steel five feet long. Without word or
hesitation he swung the sword, held in both hands,
up over the little girl's neck. The drum stopped
beating.

As the blade swung to its highest point and
poised, a figure in black darted out from the left
side of the throne, leapt down the stairs, and stayed
the sacrificer's arms with slenderer arms. The sharp
edge of the sword glittered in midair. So they bal-
anced for a moment, the white figure and the black,
both faceless, dancer-like above the motionless
child whose white neck was bared by the parting of
her black hair.

In silence each leapt aside and up the stairs
again, vanishing in the darkness behind the enormous throne. A priestess came forward and poured
out a bowl of some liquid on the steps beside the
kneeling child. The stain looked black in the dim-
ness of the hall.

The child got up and descended the four stairs
laboriously. When she stood at the bottom, the two
tall priestesses put on her a black robe and hood

and mantle, and turned her around again to face
the steps, the dark stain, the throne.

"O let the Nameless Ones behold the girl given
to them, who is verily the one born ever nameless.
Let them accept her life and the years of her life
until her death, which is also theirs. Let them find
her acceptable. Let her be eaten!"

Other voices, shrill and harsh as trumpets, replied: "She is eaten! She is eaten!"

The little girl stood looking from under her
black cowl up at the throne. The jewels inset in the
huge clawed arms and the back were glazed with
dust, and on the carven back were cobwebs and
whitish stains of owl droppings. The three highest
steps directly before the throne, above the step on
which she had knelt, had never been climbed by
mortal feet. They were so thick with dust that they
looked like one slant of grey soil, the planes of the
red-veined marble wholly hidden by the unstirred,
untrodden siftings of how many years, how many
centuries.

"She is eaten! She is eaten!"

Now the drum, abrupt, began to sound again,
beating a quicker pace.

Silent and shuffling, the procession formed and
moved away from the throne, eastward toward the
bright, distant square of the doorway. On either
side, the thick double columns, like the calves of

immense pale legs, went up to the dusk under the ceiling. Among the priestesses, and now all in black like them, the child walked, her small bare feet treading solemnly over the frozen weeds, the icy stones. When sunlight slanting through the ruined roof flashed across her way, she did not look up.

Guards held the great doors wide. The black procession came out into the thin, cold light and wind of early morning. The sun dazzled, swimming above the eastern vastness. Westward, the mountains caught its yellow light, as did the façade of the Hall of the Throne. The other buildings, lower on the hill, still lay in purplish shadow, except for the Temple of the God-Brothers across the way on a little knoll: its roof, newly gilt, flashed the day back in glory. The black line of priestesses, four by four, wound down the Hill of the Tombs, and as they went they began softly to chant. The tune was on three notes only, and the word that was repeated over and over was a word so old it had lost its meaning, like a signpost still standing when the road is gone. Over and over they chanted the empty word. All that day of the Remaking of the Priestess was filled with the low chanting of women's voices, a dry unceasing drone.

The little girl was taken from room to room, from temple to temple. In one place salt was placed upon her tongue; in another she knelt facing west while her hair was cut short and washed with oil and scented vinegar; in another she lay facedown on a slab of black marble behind an altar while shrill voices sang a lament for the dead. Neither she nor any of the priestesses ate food or drank water all that day. As the evening star set, the little girl was put to bed, naked between sheepskin rugs, in a room she had never slept in before. It was in a house that had been locked for years, unlocked only that day. The room was higher than it was long, and had no windows. There was a dead smell in it, still and stale. The silent women left her there in the dark.

She held still, lying just as they had put her. Her eyes were wide open. She lay so for a long time.

She saw light shake on the high wall. Someone came quietly along the corridor, shielding a rush-light so it showed no more light than a firefly. A husky whisper: "Ho, are you there, Tenar?"

The child did not reply.

A head poked in the doorway, a strange head, hairless as a peeled potato, and of the same yellow-ish color. The eyes were like potato-eyes, brown and tiny. The nose was dwarfed by great, flat slabs of cheek, and the mouth was a lipless slit. The child stared unmoving at this face. Her eyes were large, dark, and fixed.

"Ho, Tenar, my little honeycomb, there you are!" The voice was husky, high as a woman's voice but not a woman's voice. "I shouldn't be here, I belong outside the door, on the porch, that's where I go. But I had to see how my little Tenar is, after all the long day of it, eh, how's my poor little honeycomb?"

He moved toward her, noiseless and burly, and put out his hand as if to smooth back her hair.

"I am not Tenar anymore," the child said, staring up at him. His hand stopped; he did not touch her.

"No," he said, after a moment, whispering. "I know. I know. Now you're the little Eaten One. But I . . ."

She said nothing.

"It was a hard day for a little one," the man said, shuffling, the tiny light flickering in his big yellow hand.

"You should not be in this House, Manan."

"No. No. I know. I shouldn't be in this House. Well, good night, little one. . . . Good night."

The child said nothing. Manan slowly turned around and went away. The glimmer died from the high cell walls.

The little girl, who had no name anymore but *Arha*, the Eaten One, lay on her back looking steadily at the dark.

# CHAPTER 2

# THE WALL AROUND
# THE PLACE

**As she grew older she** lost all remembrance of her mother, without knowing she had lost it. She belonged here, at the Place of the Tombs; she had always belonged here. Only sometimes in the long evenings of July as she watched the western mountains, dry and lion-colored in the afterglow of sunset, she would think of a fire that had burned on a hearth, long ago, with the same clear yellow light. And with this came a memory of being held, which was strange, for here she was seldom even touched; and the memory of a pleasant smell, the fragrance of hair freshly washed and rinsed in sage-scented water, fair long hair, the color of sunset and firelight. That was all she had left.

She knew more than she remembered, of course, for she had been told the whole story. When she was seven or eight years old, and first beginning to wonder who indeed this person called "Arha" was, she had gone to her guardian, the Warden Manan, and said, "Tell me how I was chosen, Manan."

"Oh, you know all that, little one."

And indeed she did; the tall, dry-voiced priestess Thar had told her till she knew the words by heart, and she recited them: "Yes, I know. At the death of the One Priestess of the Tombs of Atuan, the ceremonies of burial and purification are completed within one month by the moon's calendar. After this certain of the Priestesses and Wardens of the Place of the Tombs go forth across the desert, among the towns and villages of Atuan, seeking and asking. They seek the girl-child who was born on the night of the Priestess's death. When they find such a child, they wait and they watch. The child must be sound of body and of mind, and as it grows it must not suffer from rickets nor the smallpox nor any deformity, nor become blind. If it reaches the age of five years unblemished, then it is known that the body of the child is indeed the new body of the Priestess who died. And the child is made known to the Godking in Awabath, and brought here to her Temple and instructed for a year. And at the year's end she is taken to the Hall of the Throne and her name is given back to those who are her Masters, the Nameless Ones: for she is the nameless one, the Priestess Ever Reborn."

This was all word for word as Thar had told her, and she had never dared ask for a word more. The thin priestess was not cruel, but she was very cold and lived by an iron law, and Arha was in awe of her. But she was not in awe of Manan, far from it, and she would command him, "Now tell me how *I* was chosen!" And he would tell her again.

"We left here, going north and west, in the third day of the moon's waxing; for Arha-that-was had died in the third day of the last moon. And first we went to Tenacbah, which is a great city, though those who've seen both say it's no more to Awabath than a flea to a cow. But it's big enough for me, there must be ten hundred houses in Tenacbah! And we went on to Gar. But nobody in those cities had a baby girl born to them on the third day of the moon a month before; there were some had boys, but boys won't do. . . . So we went into the hill country north of Gar, to the towns and villages. That's my own land. I was born in the hills there, where the rivers run, and the land is green. Not in this desert." Manan's husky voice would get a strange sound when he said that, and his small eyes would be quite hidden in their folds; he would pause a little, and at last go on. "And so we found and spoke to all those who were parents of babies born in the last months. And some would lie to us. 'Oh yes, surely our baby girl was born on the moon's third day!' For poor folk, you know, are often glad to get rid of girl-babies. And there were others who were so poor, living in lonely huts in the valleys of the hills, that they kept no count of days and scarce knew how to tell the turn of time, so they could not say for certain how old their baby was. But we could always come at the truth, by asking long enough. But it was slow work. At last we found a girl-child, in a village of ten houses, in the orchard-vales westward of Entat. Eight months old she was, so long had we been looking. But she had been born on the night that the Priestess of the Tombs had died, and within the very hour of her death. And she was a fine baby, sitting up on her mother's knee and looking with bright eyes at all of us, crowding into the one room of the house like bats into a cave! The father was a poor man. He tended the apple trees of the rich man's orchard, and had nothing of his own but five children and a goat. Not even the house was his. So there we all crowded in, and you could tell by the way the priestesses looked at the baby and spoke among themselves that they thought they had found the Reborn One at last. And the mother could tell this too. She held the baby and never said a word. Well, so, the next day we came back. And look here! The little bright-eyed baby lying in a cot of rushes weeping and screaming, and all over its body weals and red rashes of fever, and the mother wailing louder than the baby, 'Oh! Oh! My babe hath the Witch-Fingers on her!' That's how she said it; the smallpox she meant. In my village, too, they called it the Witch-Fingers. But Kossil, she who is

now the High Priestess of the Godking, she went to
the cot and picked up the baby. The others had all
drawn back, and I with them; I don't value my life
very high, but who enters a house where smallpox
is? But she had no fear, not that one. She picked up
the baby and said, 'It has no fever.' And she spat on
her finger and rubbed at the red marks, and they
came off. They were only berry juice. The poor
silly mother had thought to fool us and keep her
child!" Manan laughed heartily at this; his yellow
face hardly changed, but his sides heaved. "So, her
husband beat her, for he was afraid of the wrath of
the priestesses. And soon we came back to the desert,
but each year one of the people of the Place would
return to the village among the apple orchards, and
see how the child got on. So five years passed, and
then Thar and Kossil made the journey, with the
Temple guards, and soldiers of the red helmet sent
by the Godking to escort them safely. They brought
the child back here, for it was indeed the Priestess of
the Tombs reborn, and here it belonged. And who
was the child, eh, little one?"

"Me," said Arha, looking off into the distance
as if to see something she could not see, something
gone out of sight.

Once she asked, "What did the . . . the mother
do, when they came to take the child away?"

But Manan didn't know; he had not gone with the priestesses on that final journey.

And she could not remember. What was the good in remembering? It was gone, all gone. She had come where she must come. In all the world she knew only one place: the Place of the Tombs of Atuan.

In her first year there she had slept in the big dormitory with the other novices, girls between four and fourteen. Even then Manan had been set apart among the Ten Wardens as her particular guardian, and her cot had been in a little alcove, partly separated from the long, low-beamed main room of the dormitory in the Big House where the girls giggled and whispered before they slept, and yawned and plaited one another's hair in the grey light of morning. When her name was taken from her and she became Arha, she slept alone in the Small House, in the bed and in the room that would be her bed and her room for the rest of her life. That house was hers, the House of the One Priestess, and no one might enter it without her permission. When she was quite little still, she enjoyed hearing people knock submissively on her door, and saying, "You may come in," and it annoyed her that the two High Priestesses, Kossil and Thar, took their permission for granted and entered her house without knocking.

The days went by, the years went by, all alike. The girls of the Place of the Tombs spent their time at classes and disciplines. They did not play any games. There was no time for games. They learned the sacred songs and the sacred dances, the histories of the Kargad Lands, and the mysteries of whichever of the gods they were dedicated to: the Godking who ruled in Awabath, or the Twin Brothers, Atwah and Wuluah. Of them all, only Arha learned the rites of the Nameless Ones, and these were taught her by one person, Thar, the High Priestess of the Twin Gods. This took her away from the others for an hour or more daily, but most of her day, like theirs, was spent simply working. They learned how to spin and weave the wool of their flocks, and how to plant and harvest and prepare the food they always ate: lentils, buckwheat ground to a coarse meal for porridge or a fine flour for unleavened bread, onions, cabbages, goat-cheese, apples, and honey.

The best thing that could happen was to be allowed to go fishing in the murky green river that flowed through the desert a half mile northeast of the Place; to take along an apple or a cold buckwheat bannock for lunch and sit all day in the dry sunlight among the reeds, watching the slow green water run and the cloud-shadows change slowly on the mountains. But if you squealed with excitement when the line tensed and you swung in a flat, glittering fish to flop on the riverbank and drown in air, then Mebbeth would hiss like an adder, "Be still, you screeching fool!" Mebbeth, who served in the Godking's temple, was a dark woman, still young, but hard and sharp as obsidian. Fishing was her passion. You had to keep on her good side, and never make a sound, or she would not take you out to fish again; and then you'd never get to the river except to fetch water in summer when the wells ran low. That was a dreary business, to trudge through the searing white heat a half mile down to the river, fill the two buckets on their carrying pole, and then set off as fast as possible uphill to the Place. The first hundred yards were easy, but then the buckets began to grow heavier, and the pole burned your shoulders like a bar of hot iron, and the light glared on the dry road, and every step was harder and slower. At last you got to the cool shade of the back courtyard of the Big House by the vegetable patch, and dumped the buckets into the great cistern with a splash. And then you had to turn around to do it all over again, and again, and again.

Within the precincts of the Place—that was all the name it had or needed, for it was the most ancient and sacred of all places in the Four Lands of the Kargish Empire—a couple of hundred people lived, and there were many buildings: three temples, the Big House and the Small House, the quarters of the eunuch wardens, and close outside the wall the guards' barracks and many slaves' huts, the storehouses and sheep pens and goat pens and farm buildings. It looked like a little town, seen from a distance, from up on the dry hills westward where nothing grew but sage, wire-grass in straggling clumps, small weeds and desert herbs. Even from away off on the eastern plains, looking up one might see the gold roof of the Temple of the Twin Gods wink and glitter beneath the mountains, like a speck of mica in a shelf of rock.

That temple itself was a cube of stone, plastered white, windowless, with a low porch and door. Showier, and centuries newer, was the Temple of the Godking a little below it, with a high portico and a row of thick white columns with painted capitals—each one a solid log of cedar, brought on shipboard from Hur-at-Hur where there are forests, and dragged by the straining of twenty slaves across the barren plains to the Place. Only after a traveler approaching from the east had seen the gold roof and the bright columns would he see, higher up on the Hill of the Place, above them all, tawny and ruinous as the desert itself, the oldest of the temples of his race: the huge, low Hall of the Throne, with patched walls and flattish, crumbling dome.

Behind the Hall and encircling the whole crest of the hill ran a massive wall of rock, laid without mortar and half fallen down in many places. Inside the loop of the wall several black stones eighteen or twenty feet high stuck up like huge fingers out of the earth. Once the eye saw them it kept returning to them. They stood there full of meaning, and yet there was no saying what they meant. There were nine of them. One stood straight, the others leaned more or less, two had fallen. They were crusted with grey and orange lichen as if splotched with paint, all but one, which was naked and black, with a dull gloss to it. It was smooth to the touch, but on the others, under the crust of lichen, vague carvings could be seen, or felt with the fingers—shapes, signs. These nine stones were the Tombs of Atuan. They had stood there, it was said, since the time of the first men, since Earthsea was created. They had been planted in the darkness when the lands were raised up from the ocean's depths. They were older by far than the Godkings of Kargad, older than the Twin Gods, older than light. They were the tombs of those who ruled before the world of men came to be, the ones not named, and she who served them had no name.

She did not go among them often, and no one else ever set foot on that ground where they stood,

on the hilltop within the rock wall behind the
Hall of the Throne. Twice a year, at the full moon
nearest the equinox of spring and of autumn, there
was a sacrifice before the Throne and she came
out from the low back door of the Hall carrying a
great brass basin full of smoking goat's blood; this
she must pour out, half at the foot of the standing black stone, half over one of the fallen stones
which lay embedded in the rocky dirt, stained by
the blood-offering of centuries.

Sometimes Arha went by herself in the early
morning and wandered among the Stones trying
to make out the dim humps and scratches of the
carvings, brought out more clearly by the low angle
of the light; or she would sit there and look up at
the mountains westward, and down at the roofs
and walls of the Place all laid out below, and watch
the first stirrings of activity around the Big House
and the guards' barracks, and the flocks of sheep
and goats going off to their sparse pastures by the
river. There was never anything to do among the
Stones. She went only because it was permitted her
to go there, because there she was alone. It was a
dreary place. Even in the heat of noon in the desert
summer there was a coldness about it. Sometimes
the wind whistled a little between the two stones
that stood closest together, leaning together as if
telling secrets. But no secret was told.

From the Tomb Wall another, lower rock wall ran, making a long irregular semicircle about the Hill of the Place and then trailing off northward toward the river. It did not so much protect the Place, as cut it in two: on one side the temples and houses of the priestesses and wardens, on the other the quarters of the guards and of the slaves who farmed and herded and foraged for the Place. None of these ever crossed the wall, except that on certain very holy festivals the guards, and their drummers and players of the horn, would attend the procession of the priestesses; but they did not enter the portals of the temples. No other men set foot upon the inner ground of the Place. There had once been pilgrimages, kings and chieftains coming from the Four Lands to worship there; the first Godking, a century and a half ago, had come to enact the rites of his own temple. Yet even he could not enter among the Tombstones, even he had had to eat and sleep outside the wall around the Place.

One could climb that wall easily enough, fitting toes into crevices. The Eaten One and a girl called Penthe were sitting up on the wall one afternoon in late spring. They were both twelve years old. They were supposed to be in the weaving room of the Big House, a huge stone attic; they were supposed to be at the great looms always warped with dull black wool, weaving black cloth for robes. They had

slipped outside for a drink at the well in the courtyard, and then Arha had said, "Come on!" and had
led the other girl down the hill, around out of sight
of the Big House, to the wall. Now they sat on top
of it, ten feet up, their bare legs dangling down on
the outside, looking over the flat plains that went
on and on to the east and north.

"I'd like to see the sea," said Penthe.

"What for?" said Arha, chewing a bitter stem of
milkweed she had picked from the wall. The barren
land was just past its flowering. All the small desert
blossoms, yellow and rose and white, low-growing
and quick-flowering, were going to seed, scattering tiny plumes and parasols of ash white on the
wind, dropping their hooked, ingenious burrs. The
ground under the apple trees of the orchard was
a drift of bruised white and pink. The branches
were green, the only green trees within miles of
the Place. Everything else, from horizon to horizon, was a dull, tawny, desert color, except that the
mountains had a silvery bluish tinge from the first
buds of the flowering sage.

"Oh, I don't know what for. I'd just like to
see something different. It's always the same here.
Nothing happens."

"All that happens everywhere, begins here," said
Arha.

"Oh, I know. . . . But I'd like to see some of it happening!"

Penthe smiled. She was a soft, comfortable-looking girl. She scratched the soles of her bare feet on the sun-warmed rocks, and after a while went on, "You know, I used to live by the sea when I was little. Our village was right behind the dunes, and we used to go down and play on the beach sometimes. Once I remember we saw a fleet of ships going by, way out at sea. We ran and told the village and everybody came to see. The ships looked like dragons with red wings. Some of them had real necks, with dragon heads. They came sailing by Atuan, but they weren't Kargish ships. They came from the west, from the Inner Lands, the headman said. Everybody came down to watch them. I think they were afraid they might land. They just went by, nobody knew where they were going. Maybe to make war in Karego-At. But think of it, they really came from the sorcerers' islands, where all the people are the color of dirt and they can all cast a spell on you easy as winking."

"Not on me," Arha said fiercely. "I wouldn't have looked at them. They're vile accursed sorcerers. How dare they sail so close to the Holy Land?"

"Oh, well, I suppose the Godking will conquer

them someday and make them all slaves. But I wish I could see the sea again. There used to be little octopuses in the tide pools, and if you shouted 'Boo!' at them they turned all white.—There comes that old Manan, looking for you."

Arha's guard and servant was coming slowly along the inner side of the wall. He would stoop to pull a wild onion, of which he held a large, limp bunch, then straighten up and look about him with his small, dull, brown eyes. He had grown fatter with the years, and his hairless yellow skin glistened in the sun.

"Slide down part way on the men's side," Arha hissed, and both girls wriggled lithe as lizards down the far side of the wall until they could cling there just below the top, invisible from the inner side. They heard Manan's slow footsteps coming by.

"Hoo! Hoo! Potato face!" crooned Arha, a whispering jeer faint as the wind among the grasses.

The heavy tread halted. "Ho there," said the uncertain voice. "Little one? Arha?"

Silence.

Manan went forward.

"Hoo-oo! Potato face!"

"Hoo, potato belly!" Penthe whispered in imitation, and then moaned, trying to suppress giggles.

"Somebody there?"

Silence.

"Oh well, well, well," the eunuch sighed, and his slow feet went on. When he was gone over the shoulder of the slope, the girls scrambled back up onto the top of the wall. Penthe was pink with sweat and giggles, but Arha looked savage.

"The stupid old bellwether, following me around everywhere!"

"He has to," Penthe said reasonably. "It's his job, looking after you."

"Those I serve look after me. I please them; I need please nobody else. These old women and half-men, these people should leave me alone. I am the One Priestess!"

Penthe stared at the other girl. "Oh," she said feebly, "oh, I know you are, Arha—"

"Then they should let me be. And not order me about all the time!"

Penthe said nothing for a while, but sighed, and sat swinging her plump legs and gazing at the vast, pale lands below, that rose so slowly to a high, vague, immense horizon.

"You'll get to give the orders pretty soon, you know," she said at last, quietly. "In two more years we won't be children anymore. We'll be fourteen. I'll go into the Godking's temple, and things will be about the same for me. But you'll really be the High Priestess then. Even Kossil and Thar will have to obey you."

The Eaten One said nothing. Her face was set, her eyes under black brows caught the light of the sky in a pale glitter.

"We ought to go back," Penthe said.

"No."

"But the weaving mistress might tell Thar. And soon it'll be time for the Nine Chants."

"I'm staying here. You stay, too."

"They won't punish you, but they will punish me," Penthe said in her mild way. Arha did not reply. Penthe sighed, and stayed. The sun was sinking into haze high above the plains. Far away on the long, gradual slant of the land, sheep bells clanked faintly and lambs bleated. The spring wind blew in dry, faint gusts, sweet-smelling.

The Nine Chants were nearly over when the two girls returned. Mebbeth had seen them sitting on the "Men's Wall" and had reported this to her superior, Kossil, High Priestess of the Godking.

Kossil was heavy-footed, heavy-faced. Without expression in face or voice she spoke to the two girls, telling them to follow her. She led them through the stone hallways of the Big House, out the front door, up the knoll to the Temple of Atwah and Wuluah. There she spoke with the High Priestess of that temple, Thar, tall and dry and thin as the legbone of a deer.

Kossil said to Penthe, "Take off your gown."

She whipped the girl with a bundle of reed canes, which cut the skin a little. Penthe bore this patiently, with silent tears. She was sent back to the weaving room without supper, and the next day also she would go without food. "If you are found climbing over the Men's Wall again," Kossil said, "there will be very much worse things than this happen to you. Do you understand, Penthe?" Kossil's voice was soft, but not kindly. Penthe said, "Yes," and slipped away, cowering and flinching as her heavy clothing rubbed the cuts on her back.

Arha had stood beside Thar to watch the whipping. Now she watched Kossil clean the canes of the whip.

Thar said to her, "It is not fitting that you be seen climbing and running with other girls. You are Arha."

She stood sullen and did not reply.

"It is better that you do only what is needful for you to do. You are Arha."

For a moment the girl raised her eyes to Thar's face, then to Kossil's, and there was a depth of hate or rage in her look that was terrible to see. But the thin priestess showed no concern; rather she confirmed, leaning forward a little, almost whispering, "*You are Arha*. There is nothing left. It was all eaten."

"It was all eaten," the girl repeated, as she had repeated daily, all the days of her life since she was six.

Thar bowed her head slightly; so did Kossil, as she put away the whip. The girl did not bow, but turned submissively and left.

After the supper of potatoes and spring onions, eaten in silence in the narrow, dark refectory, after the chanting of the evening hymns, and the placing of the sacred words upon the doors, and the brief Ritual of the Unspoken, the work of the day was done. Now the girls might go up to the dormitory and play games with dice and sticks, so long as the single rushlight burned, and whisper in the dark from bed to bed. Arha set off across the courts and slopes of the Place as she did every night, to the Small House where she slept alone.

The night wind was sweet. The stars of spring shone thick, like drifts of daisies in spring meadows, like the glittering of light on the April sea. But the girl had no memory of meadows or the sea. She did not look up.

"Ho there, little one!"

"Manan," she said indifferently.

The big shadow shuffled up beside her, starlight glinting on his hairless pate.

"Were you punished?"

"I can't be punished."

"No. . . . That's so. . . ."

"They can't punish me. They don't dare."

He stood with his big hands hanging, dim and bulky. She smelled wild onion, and the sweaty, sagey smell of his old black robes, which were torn at the hem, and too short for him.

"They can't touch me. I am Arha," she said in a shrill, fierce voice, and burst into tears.

The big, waiting hands came up and drew her to him, held her gently, smoothed her braided hair. "There, there. Little honeycomb, little girl. . . ." She heard the husky murmur in the deep hollow of his chest, and clung to him. Her tears stopped soon, but she held on to Manan as if she could not stand up.

"Poor little one," he whispered, and picking the child up carried her to the doorway of the house where she slept alone. He set her down.

"All right now, little one?"

She nodded, turned from him, and entered the dark house.

**URSULA K. LE GUIN** is one of the most distinguished fantasy and science fiction writers of all time. She has won numerous awards for her work, including the Nebula Award, the Hugo Award, the National Book Award, and the Newbery Honor. She lives in Portland, Oregon. Visit her online at ursulakleguin.com.